THE PET FINDERS CLUB

THE PET FINDERS CLUB

THE PET FINDERS CLUB

Help Honey!

AS	Dumfries and Galloway LIBRARIES	
	0 2 4 1 0 1	Class JF

BEN M. BAGLIO

Hodder
Children's
Books

A division of Hachette Children's Books

Special thanks to Liss Norton

Text copyright © 2006 Working Partners Ltd
Illustration copyright © 2008 Cecilia Johansson

First published in the USA in 2006 by Scholastic Inc

First published in Great Britain in 2008
by Hodder Children's Books

The rights of Ben M Baglio and Cecilia Johansson to be
identified as the Author and Illustrator of the Work respectively
have been asserted by them in accordance with the
Copyright, Designs and Patents Act 1988

1

All rights reserved. Apart from any use permitted under
UK copyright law, this publication may only be reproduced,
stored or transmitted, in any form, or by any means with prior
permission in writing from the publishers or in the case of
reprographic production in accordance with the terms of
licences issued by the Copyright Licensing Agency and may
not be otherwise circulated in any form of binding or cover
other than that in which it is published and without a similar
condition being imposed on the subsequent purchaser.

All characters in this publication are fictitious and any resemblance
to real persons, living or dead, is purely coincidental.

ISBN-13: 978 0 340 93139 4

Typeset in Weiss by Avon DataSet Ltd,
Bidford on Avon, Warwickshire

Printed and bound in Great Britain by
CPI Bookmarque, Croydon, CR0 4TD

The paper and board used in this paperback by Hodder Children's
Books are natural recyclable products made from wood grown in
sustainable forests. The manufacturing processes conform to the
environmental regulations of the country of origin.

Hodder Children's Books
a division of Hachette Children's Books
338 Euston Road, London NW1 3BH
An Hachette Livre UK Company

Chapter One

"Jet's doing brilliantly, isn't he, Buddy?" Andi Talbot said to her cute tan-and-white Jack Russell terrier. She and Buddy were watching the Basic Obedience class at the RSPCA centre in Aldcliffe, a suburb of Lancaster, while they waited for their Musical Freestyling lesson to begin.

Andi's friend, Natalie, and her black Labrador, Jet, had been attending the Obedience class for a few months, and Andi could really see the difference in Jet's behaviour. The owners were lining up their dogs along the far side of the hall. Jet was in the middle of the line, watching Natalie intently.

"Sit, Jet," Natalie said.

Jet obediently folded his haunches underneath him. Natalie unclipped his lead, gave him the command to stay, and walked away. The other dogs scampered after their owners but Jet stayed put.

"That's terrific, Natalie!" Fisher Pearce called from the other end of the hall. He was the tall, good-looking RSPCA vet who ran the Obedience classes. "When you think what he used to be like . . .!"

"Don't remind her!" Andi grinned at Natalie, who rolled her eyes. It was hard to believe that not long ago Natalie couldn't let Jet off his lead because he'd probably have run off and got lost. In fact, it was after one of Jet's solo adventures that Andi and Nat had become friends.

Buddy had got lost too, and while Andi and her friend, Tristan, were searching for him, they'd found Jet! Soon after, the three of them formed the Pet Finders Club and together they had solved loads of missing-animal cases.

Natalie reached the far side of the hall and turned back to Jet. "Here, boy," she called, patting her legs. Jet charged towards her, bounding over a plump Pekingese. He launched himself at Natalie and sent her staggering back against the wall.

"Whoa!" Natalie laughed. When she'd regained her balance she patted the panting dog's neck. "Good boy, Jet. But you could try being a bit less enthusiastic next time."

Fisher clapped his hands. "Can I have everyone's attention, please?"

The dog-owners clipped leads on to their pets then turned towards Fisher.

"Christine Wilson from Paws for Thought should be here any minute now with entry forms for the first ever Aldcliffe Pet Show. I hope you'll all enter your dogs, and any other pets you might— Ah, here she is!"

Christine was backing into the hall carrying one end of a heavy box with the other end held by Tristan.

Andi felt a thrill of excitement. Christine and Fisher had been working out the details of the show for weeks. It was part of a national programme of shows sponsored by the RSPCA and had even been advertised on TV, to attract people with pedigree

3

pets who were regulars on the show circuit. Now, at last, she'd find out all about Aldcliffe's event. "Come on, Bud," she said, darting across the hall to help.

"Please pick up leaflets and entry forms as you leave. I'll see you all next week," Fisher told the students. "Natalie, can I see you for a moment?"

"OK." Natalie crossed the room with Jet by her side.

Tristan and Christine lowered the box of pet show details on to a table near the door. "Ow," Tristan said, blowing on his hands. "I never realized paper could be so heavy."

People began to gather round the table, and Andi grabbed a handful of leaflets to give out.

"There's a Basic Obedience class in the show," Christine said to the dog-owners. "Perhaps some of you would like to enter that one. There's a class for the prettiest dog, too, as well as the more usual pet show classes for pedigrees, of course. The RSPCA wants to give people with ordinary pets the chance to compete alongside serious entrants so that everyone sees how much fun pet shows can be."

Andi gave out the last of her leaflets, then

grabbed one for herself. There were so many classes; she wasn't sure which was the best one for Buddy to enter.

Tristan read the list over her shoulder. "Nothing for snakes or reptiles," he said, disappointed. "That's a shame. That would have been worth seeing."

"They'll all be worth seeing," Andi pointed out.

Natalie came racing over with Jet at her heels. "Guess what? Jet's been promoted to the Intermediate Obedience Class!"

"That's amazing!" Tristan cried.

"Good old Jet!" Andi exclaimed, patting him. "Hey, Nat. You should try this event – the Junior Dog-Handler category." She pointed to a line on her flyer. "And Tris, your cat, Lucy, should go in for the cat competition."

"I'll think about it," Tristan replied. "But she gets loads of attention already from being in cat-food adverts – any more, and she might start acting like a film star!"

"I think Jet and Buddy should both enter the Junior Dog-Handling," Fisher said, coming over.

"Me too," Christine agreed, tucking a lock of

dark hair behind her ear. "The show organizers are especially keen for young people to get involved, which is why they've provided some special classes. You'll have to walk your dogs around the floor at different speeds, get them to change direction, walk to heel . . . that sort of thing."

"Buddy could definitely do that," Andi said, making up her mind to put his name down.

Natalie shook her head. "I don't know if Jet's ready to perform in front of strangers."

"He'll be fine," Fisher said. "And the judges will be looking at how the handlers work their dogs. They won't expect polished show-ring performances."

"We're going to get each dog to do a little trick, too," Christine continued.

Andi had never tried teaching Buddy a trick before, but she didn't see why he couldn't learn one for the show. In fact, teaching him would be fun. "Buddy would love that."

Natalie frowned. "That sounds hard." She took the leaflet from Andi and scanned it. "Now *this* is perfect for Jet: Best Condition Dog. Hasn't he got the glossiest fur you've ever seen?"

"The judges won't be looking only at a dog's appearance," Fisher said. "They'll want to see how well he interacts with you. And how well he behaves while he's being shown."

Chloe, the Musical Freestyling teacher, entered the hall with Purdy, her cream Pomeranian. "Hello, everyone. Has Fisher told you about the Freestyling demonstration I'm giving at the pet show?"

"Nope," Andi and Natalie said together.

Chloe stopped beside them. She made a tiny gesture with her hand and Purdy instantly sat at her feet. "I hoped you two would take part," she said.

"Cool!" Andi exclaimed. She and Buddy loved Musical Freestyling, which was like dancing for dogs. "Come on, Nat! You and Jet have got to do it too. It'll be so much fun!"

Buddy barked twice.

"OK!" Natalie grinned. "I can see Buddy means business."

Then a smartly-dressed man with light-brown skin and friendly brown eyes entered the hall. A tiny ball of golden fluff trotted in behind him.

"Oh wow!" Andi cried when she saw them. "What sort of dog is she?" She knelt beside the tiny creature and held out her hand to be sniffed.

"A long-haired chihuahua," the man said.

Andi ran her hand gently over the tiny dog's soft fur. "Aren't you cute?" she whispered. The dog wasn't much bigger than one of Andi's mum's fluffy slippers. Her thick fur was mostly golden tan but her nose, chest and paws were pure white. Her gorgeous dark eyes gazed up at Andi.

"Hello, Fisher," said the chihuahua's owner. "I've come to pick up a pet show entry form."

"Excellent!" Fisher said. "I hoped you'd enter. Kids, this is David Nazrallah. These three are the Pet Finders: Andi, Tristan and Natalie. If you ever lose a pet, they're the people to see." He stooped down and ran his fingers along the chihuahua's back. "This little lady is Supreme Champion High Ridge Honeybee."

"Honey for short," David said.

Andi thought the name suited the dog perfectly: her fur was the exact colour of honey.

Natalie slid on to the floor beside Andi. "I've

8

never seen a dog this small before. How old is she, Mr Nazrallah?"

"Almost two. And call me David."

Natalie stroked one of Honey's ears. "She's even softer than that angora jumper I bought last week."

Jet reached down to sniff the chihuahua. "Careful, Jet," Natalie warned. She gently pushed him away. "You'll frighten Honey."

"It's OK," David said. "She loves other dogs."

The little dog boldly trotted up to Jet, reaching up to sniff him. Jet lowered his head and touched her nose with his. Buddy just stared at Honey as though trying to work out what sort of animal she could possibly be.

"Jet looks like a giant next to Honey," Tristan said. "And even Buddy seems big. I bet you could carry Honey around in your pocket if you wanted to."

"Not quite," David laughed. "Actually she travels in a dog-carrier. I asked Christine for something a bit out of the ordinary and she came up with a fabulous sparkly pink carrier. It's a bit over the top, but Honey deserves it."

"Does Honey win lots of shows?" Andi asked.

She was starting to feel a bit anxious about entering Buddy for the pet show now she knew that Honey would be taking part: Buddy was the best dog in the world but he wasn't exactly showy.

"Quite a few," David said.

Chloe glanced at her watch. "I'd better get started. Can I interest you and Honey in Musical Freestyling, David?"

"No thanks. It's not really our thing," he replied. "Well, great to meet you all. Come on, Honey." He strode away with the chihuahua trotting daintily behind him.

"I didn't realize top show-dogs would be entering the pet show," Andi remarked as Chloe headed to the far end of the hall to prepare for the Freestyling lesson. "Buddy's not a show-dog. Perhaps I shouldn't enter him."

"Of course you should," Christine said firmly. "The judge will love his personality. And anyway, Honey and Buddy won't be in the same class." She ruffled Buddy's fur. "If you want to make him look extra good, you can always take him to Clip 'n' Curl."

11

"Clip 'n' Curl?" Andi echoed.

"It's the new pet-grooming parlour just off the high street. A friend of mine runs it. She used to be a hairdresser but she likes dogs and cats better than people so now she pampers them instead. Her name's Aggie Patel."

"What about a makeover, Buddy?" Andi asked.

"I'll take Jet," Natalie decided. "He'll look perfect in the show-ring if he's been groomed by an expert. Hey, perhaps my mum will make me a few appointments at her beauty salon so I look good, too."

"Uh-oh," Tristan muttered. "Something tells me Nat's about to get carried away with grooming."

"Don't worry. I don't want Jet and me to have matching manicures or anything. The idea of putting nail varnish on a dog's claws is totally gross. I mean, what's the point? Jet would probably chip his in seconds!" Natalie winked at Andi as Tristan looked totally horrified at the thought of canine manicures.

Chapter Two

"I can't believe summer is over already!" Andi said the next morning as she, Natalie and Tristan walked to school for the first day of the new year.

"Don't remind me," Tristan said. "I've been trying to forget."

"I bought some new combats last week," Andi said. "They're really cool. A sort of sand colour with massive pockets on the legs."

Natalie linked arms with her. "They sound great. You'll have to come over and see my new jumper. It's orange with a black stripe running down each sleeve."

As they turned into the school playground, Tristan gave an exaggerated yawn. "Clothes are so boring!"

"They're better than *skateboards*," Natalie said, digging him in the ribs. The first bell was ringing and people were already lining up.

"Who's that?" Tristan asked, pointing to a girl standing alone on the far side of the playground. "I don't recognize her. Do you think she's new?"

"Probably," Andi agreed. "She's not wearing school uniform." The girl was tall and slim with dark-brown wavy hair pulled into a high ponytail. She was dressed in a flared raspberry-pink skirt, a black top dotted with shiny white stars and a pair of black knee-length boots. A pure white fleece was slung over her arm.

"I love her outfit!" Natalie cried, pulling Andi towards the girl. "Let's find out where she buys her clothes."

Tristan groaned. "Not more fashion talk."

"Hello," Natalie called. "I like your clothes."

The girl smiled. "Really? Thanks! I had trouble deciding what to wear. I wanted to make a good impression on my first day, especially as my mum's buying my new school uniform today. This is the only chance I'll have to look good."

"You look fantastic," Natalie said. "Where did you—?"

The girl didn't let her finish. "I'm Ella Caine, by the way. Mr Robinson is my teacher. Can you show me where to go?"

"I'll show you," Tristan offered. "I'm in Mr Robinson's class this year."

"Thanks." Ella beamed at him. "Do any of you live near Oriole Way? We moved there two days ago and it would be nice to meet someone to walk to school with."

"Do you live in that big house at the end of the road?" Tristan asked, and Ella nodded. "My parents sold that. They run an estate agent's."

"Cool!" Ella did a little jump, setting her ponytail swinging. "My dad's just got a new job running the multiplex cinema in Aldcliffe. We used to live in Portsmouth. What are your names?"

Andi introduced herself and her friends. "Don't worry about being new," she added. "I started here a year ago and I was really worried on my first day. Luckily I met up with Nat and Tris and we became great friends. We even started

15

the Pet Finders Club to help people who've lost their pets."

"Yeah, we're—" Natalie began.

"I *love* animals," Ellie interrupted. "I was an RSPCA volunteer in Portsmouth. All those sweet little puppies and kittens."

"It's a pity you weren't in our class last year," Andi said. "We had a little hamster called Cinnamon—"

"A hamster!" Ella cut in. "I love their little twinkling eyes and tiny paws."

"I suppose we ought to go in," Andi said, noticing that the playground was almost empty.

"Lead on, Tristan." Ella grabbed his arm and yanked him towards the building.

Tristan glanced back at Andi and Natalie and gave them a goofy smile. "She's nice, right?" he mouthed.

Andi nodded her agreement. "Ella *is* nice," she said to Natalie when the others were out of earshot. "What do you think?"

Natalie shrugged. "She's got good fashion sense, but she talks a lot!"

* * *

16

Natalie and Andi's new classroom was large and sunny and overlooked the playing field. They found two empty spaces near the window and sat down.

Tanya McLennan, one of their classmates, was sitting at the next table. "What do you think the new teacher will be like?" she asked Andi.

Andi shrugged. "I don't know."

"Well, I hope she's young and pretty," Natalie said. "Not like Mrs Swanson. We're so lucky not to have her."

"Yes," Andi agreed. She'd heard horror stories about Mrs Swanson from Tristan's older brother, Dean.

One of Andi's classmates, Chen, turned in his seat to speak to her. "I heard that our new teacher doesn't come from round here."

Tanya nodded. "She can't be from Aldcliffe or she'd have come in last July to meet us."

"Perhaps she's from Mars or something," Larissa joked. "Any minute now, a hideous green monster will burst through the door!"

"Or maybe she'll be an alien *in disguise*," Andi countered, "who *looks* like a teacher but is really wearing loads of make-up to hide her green scaly skin."

"Good morning, everyone." The new teacher strode into the classroom and shut the door behind her. She had bright blue eyes and glossy black hair that reached almost to her waist.

"I hope she didn't hear what I said," Andi whispered to Nat.

The teacher set a pile of books down on her desk and gazed at the class. "I'm Ms McNicholas." She waited until everyone was settled then added, "I'm sorry to disappoint you all, but I am *not* an alien in disguise." Her eyes rested briefly on Andi.

Andi gulped. She *had* heard!

The classroom door opened and Howard struggled into the room carrying a bulging carrier bag. "Sorry I'm late," he said. "The strap on my rucksack broke just as I was leaving, and I had to put everything in this carrier bag instead."

"There are no excuses in this classroom," Ms McNicholas said. "Make sure you're on time tomorrow. I'm Ms McNicholas. Now, hurry up and find a free seat."

Howard turned beetroot-red. "Yes, Ms McNicholas." At that moment, his carrier bag split and pens, pencils and an apple went shooting across the floor. Andi got up to help him.

"Did I give you permission to get out of your seat?" Ms McNicholas called.

Embarrassed, Andi slid back down. She and Natalie exchanged surprised glances.

"Looks like we'll have to watch our step with her," Natalie whispered.

Andi nodded. Ms McNicholas might be young and pretty but she didn't have the same relaxed approach as their last teacher, Mr Dixon!

Chapter Three

"It's bad luck having a horrible teacher like Ms McNicholas," Tristan said as he, Andi, Natalie and Ella headed for Clip 'n' Curl after school. "Mr Robinson seems OK so far."

"He does," Ella agreed. "He's just like my old teacher back in Portsmouth – always joking and making everything seem really interesting. And he hasn't given us any homework yet."

"Lucky you," Andi sighed. "Ms McNicholas has already given us loads."

"Come on, no more talking about school," Tristan said. "When we've finished looking round Clip 'n' Curl, we should give Ella a guided tour of Aldcliffe. We'll start at Paws for Thought."

"What's that?" Ella asked.

"The best pet shop in Lancaster," Natalie replied.

"You can meet Max, the owner's spaniel," Andi put in.

"Um . . . great!" Ella said. "You should come to my dad's multiplex. It's got a twelve-screen cinema, bowling and loads of fast-food restaurants."

"Films, bowling and fast food under one roof. Heaven!" Tristan declared.

A few minutes later they were standing outside the grooming parlour, a brightly-lit place with pet accessories displayed in the window.

"Look at that!" Natalie exclaimed, pointing to a pink dog collar studded with sparkly heart-shaped gems.

Tristan laughed. "Jet would hate it. Other dogs would tease him."

Andi pressed her nose to the window. Inside she could see a spacious room with dove-grey walls, a wooden floor and shiny chrome light fittings. The wall opposite the window was covered with mirrors. Three people – two women and an older man – were grooming dogs at high tables. They were all wearing purple overalls. A raised bath stood in one corner. At the back of the shop was a waiting area where a few people were sitting with their pets.

Andi felt a thrill of excitement at the thought of picking up some tips for grooming Buddy. "Let's go in."

Ella glanced at her watch. "Oh no! I've got to go. I promised I'd babysit for my baby brother while my mum goes shopping."

"Can't you come in for a few minutes?" Andi asked. "You'll miss all the dogs."

"No, sorry. See you tomorrow." Ella sped away.

"Bye!" Tristan called as Andi led the way inside.

"I'll be with you in two seconds," one woman called as she lifted a smooth-coated dachshund down from a table and walked it across to the waiting area.

"This place is very chic," Natalie observed. "It reminds me of the hair salon I go to with my mum."

"Well, you'd better make sure you're in the right place next time you get your hair cut," Tristan joked, "or you might end up with a show clip."

"Sorry to keep you waiting," the woman said, walking over to them. She was small and slim and had dark hair pulled into a low bun.

"Are you Aggie?" Tristan asked.

"That's right." Aggie's smile grew broader. "Would you like to book a grooming session?" She opened a large appointment book that lay on a wide glass shelf in an arch-topped alcove. The phone began to ring, but Aggie let the answer machine take the call.

"I think so," Natalie said. "But we hoped to have a look round first. Christine Wilson told us about you."

"Then you must be the Pet Finders. I've heard all about you." Aggie gestured around the room. "This is the salon and waiting area." She pointed to a purple velvet curtain that covered a doorway. "The storerooms and kennels are out the back."

"Kennels?" Tristan echoed, surprised. "Do you board dogs here?"

"No, but some people drop off their dogs at the beginning of the day, on their way to work, and collect them later when the job's done. We need somewhere to keep the dogs while they're not being groomed."

Aggie headed for the waiting area. A stack of pet magazines was piled on a glass table in the corner and a vase containing an arrangement of dried flowers stood on a shelf above. An elderly lady sat in a white leather chair, reading a magazine, while a cute West Highland white terrier snoozed at her feet. A middle-aged man with a chocolate Labrador sat beside her. Next to him, a teenage girl was putting a tartan coat on the dachshund Aggie had just groomed.

Before Andi could decide which dog to stroke first, Aggie said, "I'm ready for Cuddles now, Mrs Granger." She took the Westie's lead. "Come on, fella."

Andi gave up on her idea of getting to know the waiting-area dogs. She didn't want to miss out on seeing exactly what went on in a grooming parlour. "Do you mind if we watch?" she asked.

"Not at all." Aggie introduced the group to Joe and Lena, the other two groomers. Joe was an older man with short grey hair, wire-framed glasses and a friendly smile. Lena, a young black woman who had braided hair caught in a thick ponytail, looked more serious.

Joe was brushing a massive St Bernard. Loose hair flew up from the dog's coat with every brush stroke and he caught it expertly with the brush before it could settle on her fur again. The St Bernard was standing perfectly still with her eyes shut.

"Daphne's a regular," Aggie explained. "Luckily, she's happy to get herself into the bath, because she's much too heavy for anyone to lift."

Andi glanced at the bath and saw that a set of steps led up to the far end of it. She wished they'd come earlier: it would have been great to see the huge St Bernard jumping into the water.

At the second table Lena was clipping the toenails of a young collie with a shiny brown-and-white coat.

"Doesn't that hurt?" Natalie queried as the clippers clicked and a shard of claw dropped on to the table.

"She wouldn't be so calm if it did," Lena said. "You have to clip the very end of the claw, so you don't cut the blood vessel inside the nail. Then she doesn't feel a thing." She finished the collie's last nail. "Good girl, Ruby. Now for your bow." Rows of silky ribbons were displayed at the end of each workstation. Lena snipped off a length of blue ribbon and tied it loosely around Ruby's neck so that it hid the dog's collar. Then she snapped on the collie's lead and lifted her down from the table.

The collie stood in front of a mirror gazing at her reflection. Her tail wagged from side to side; Andi wondered if Ruby knew she looked beautiful, or if she was simply happy because she'd had such a good time at the salon. She crouched down to smooth the collie's velvety fur. Ruby turned her head and licked Andi's cheek. Then she looked back at the mirror again.

"OK, that's enough staring at yourself," Lena said. "We don't want you getting conceited, do we, girl?"

"Bye, Ruby," Andi said as Lena led the collie out to the kennels.

"Bath time for you, Cuddles," Aggie said, tying on a plastic apron. She unhooked the Westie's collar and lead and lifted him into the bath, which held about twenty centimetres of warm foamy water.

Cuddles sat down, looking very contented. "He loves his bath," Aggie said. "It's a shame they're not all as easy as Cuddles. Sometimes we end up wetter than the dogs."

"Can we help you wash him?" said Tristan.

"Yes, please. There are spare aprons in the cupboard next to the bath."

The kids put them on and gathered round the bath.

"First, we have to rub right through his fur all the way down to his skin to loosen the dirt. You'd be amazed at how dirty dogs get, even stay-at-homes like Cuddles."

The Pet Finders massaged the little dog gently. His tail wagged under the foamy water.

"Well done!" Aggie said, after a few minutes. She pressed a button on the shower attachment and a spray of warm water squirted out.

"Can I rinse him?" Andi asked eagerly. This was

the part of his bath that Buddy liked best: he made a great game of trying to bite the shower spray.

"OK." Aggie pulled out the plug and the water began to drain away. Andi held the shower above Cuddles and let it rinse off the soapsuds. He sat very still with his eyes closed. "All done, boy," Andi declared, when every last bubble had been washed off.

"Thanks," Aggie said as Andi switched off the shower. "Now out you come, Cuddles." She wrapped a fluffy white towel round him, lifted him out of the tub and carried him to a grooming station. The Pet Finders helped rub him dry. Cuddles looked at each of them and gave a happy little yap.

When his fur was dry and sticking out all over the place, Aggie dropped the damp towels into a chrome laundry bin under her table. Then she selected a wide-toothed comb from her rack of grooming tools. "First I'll comb him all over," she said, letting the Westie sniff the comb before she started.

Andi watched carefully as Aggie teased out the

tangles. She combed and brushed Buddy regularly but she wanted to learn any new techniques that could help him look his best for the pet show.

Lena came back with the chocolate-brown Labrador from the waiting area, but Andi hardly noticed. She was too busy watching what Aggie was doing.

Once Cuddles was tangle-free, Aggie chose a rubber brush. "Different dogs need different brushes," she explained. "Cuddles has short hair and sensitive skin so I only use a rubber brush on him." She began to work from the little Westie's head towards his tail and legs. "It's important to go right down to the skin when you brush an animal," she said. "It stimulates the skin and allows natural oils to circulate into their coat. That way their fur stays healthy and shiny." She paused for a moment and parted the hair on Cuddles's left shoulder. "He had a patch of flaky skin here last time he came, but it seems to have gone now."

Cuddles's tail wagged non-stop while he was being groomed. He was obviously having a great time.

"There," Aggie said, setting the brush down on the table. "He doesn't need his nails clipped," she added, "because I did them only a couple of weeks ago. So it's just ears now."

Taking a cotton-wool ball from a jar on a shelf underneath the table, she moistened it with olive oil. Then she cleaned gently inside Cuddles's ear. "Do you do that every time?" Andi asked. She'd never used oil on Buddy's ears before.

Aggie nodded. "Olive oil is a great cleanser."

Andi made up her mind to try it out on Buddy. She was sure he'd enjoy the extra attention. She turned to look at the ribbons, wondering which colour Aggie would pick for the finishing touch. *Red would be nice with Cuddles's white fur*, she thought. Suddenly she noticed an array of pet costumes hanging on a rail behind the ribbon stand. "Look at these," she said, going closer.

Natalie and Tristan followed her.

"Oh, wow!" Natalie held up a doggy sailor suit and hat. "Buddy would love this!"

Tristan snorted. "Yeah, right. He'd go and roll in a muddy puddle because he was so embarrassed."

Andi laughed. Tristan was probably right. There was nothing Buddy liked more than rolling in mud but, all the same, he'd look adorable with the little sailor hat perched on his head.

"Look at this," Natalie said, holding up a pink ballerina outfit. "And *this*." She showed them a silver fairy outfit with shimmering wings.

"Don't even think about it," Andi said. "Jet would hate wearing those."

"I suppose they *are* a bit over the top," Natalie agreed.

"Over the top and down the other side!" Tristan exclaimed.

"Cuddles is finished now," Aggie called. "Would one of you like to take him to the waiting area for me while I sterilize my tools?" He was still sitting on the table but now he was wearing his collar and lead and a red ribbon tied in a neat bow.

"I'll do it," Tristan said, "before these two start dressing him up."

Aggie smiled. "Actually, our outfits are pretty popular. Quite a few of our clients hold doggy fancy-dress parties."

Tristan rolled his eyes. "I really hope you're joking," he said and led Cuddles back to his owner.

"Perhaps we can help you out, Aggie," Natalie suggested. "You said you were really busy at the moment. We could wash dogs for you and fetch them from the waiting area and the kennels, while you concentrate on grooming."

Andi couldn't think of a better way to spend her afternoons. Right now they didn't have any missing-pet cases to investigate, but working at Clip 'n' Curl would be the next best thing. They'd get to meet loads of new dogs and perhaps a few cats, too.

"That would be fantastic!" Aggie said. "And in return, I'll groom your pets for you just before the pet show."

Andi couldn't believe their luck. They'd have a great time helping out, and Bud, Jet and Lucy would get a free beauty treatment!

Chapter Four

"Come on, Buddy. Just do it once, OK?" Andi begged. It was Friday morning before school and she had been standing in her living room holding a sparkly purple hoop for over an hour. She was trying to teach her dog to jump through it for his special pet show trick. So far, it wasn't working.

"Woof!" Buddy wagged his stumpy tail.

"Go on," Andi said, pushing her hand through the hoop to show him what to do. "Good boy. You can do it."

The little Jack Russell darted forward then ducked underneath the hoop with an excited bark.

Andi lowered the hoop a little. "You've got to go *through* it, not underneath."

But Buddy didn't go underneath this time; he dodged round the side!

Andi groaned and rested the hoop on the floor. She took a dog treat out of her pocket and threw it through the hoop. "Come on, you can do it, Bud."

Buddy trotted up to the hoop and stepped through. He gobbled up the dog treat.

"You did it!" Andi whooped. She patted the little terrier and he circled round her legs.

"Now, a bit higher." Andi held the hoop slightly above the ground. "Go on, Bud." She tossed a dog treat through again.

Buddy scampered up to the hoop. He stopped and looked up at Andi. "Go on," Andi encouraged him.

Buddy sniffed the hoop then walked round it to get his treat.

"Oh, Bud!" Andi dropped the hoop.

Before Buddy could try again, the doorbell rang. "Here's Nat and Tristan," Andi said, ruffling Buddy's ears. "We'll practise again after dinner if I don't have too much homework. I'm not sure the judges will be impressed with a dog who *walks* through hoops, even if he is the best dog in the world."

"Thank goodness Ella's not in our class," Natalie said, flopping into her chair at school a little while later.

When Andi had opened her front door that morning, she'd found a smiling Tristan and Ella, and a frowning Natalie, standing outside. They'd come to walk to school with her.

"Why did Tristan have to invite her to walk with us, anyway?" Nat continued. "Who cares if he likes her? I mean, the girl won't let anyone else get a word in. I bet she's still talking Tristan's ear off right now!"

Ella did talk a lot, but Andi had a feeling that Natalie was more annoyed at all the attention the new girl was getting.

Before Andi could say anything, Ms McNicholas arrived. "Phew, it's hot in here! Let's open the windows," she said.

Andi helped open the windows while Ms McNicholas took the register.

"OK." Ms McNicholas clapped her hands. "Let's get out our history books. Today we're going to start our new topic on the Victorians."

Andi grabbed her history book and a pen from her drawer and sat down again.

"I want to tell you about Charles Dickens . . ." the teacher began.

"He's so cool!" Chen cried out.

"Well . . . I suppose you could say he was cool," Ms McNicholas said. "Dickens wrote about the living conditions of—"

"No, not him, Ms McNicholas." Chen shook his head. "*Him!*" He pointed out of the window.

Andi instantly spotted what Chen had seen – a beautiful grey parrot with bright-red tail feathers swooping across the playground. "Wow!" she gasped.

The bird made a sharp turn and headed straight for the building. It flew closer . . . and closer . . . until . . . suddenly Andy heard a fluttering noise at the open window – and the bird flew right into the classroom. "Aak . . . aak, aak!"

"Help!" Tanya yelled. Then the whole class leapt

out of their seats, shouting and laughing at once.

"Where did it come from?" someone cried.

"Catch it!" another yelled.

The parrot fluttered round the room, squawking loudly. Andi watched it excitedly, hoping it would perch on her desk. But the bird didn't settle anywhere. It soared right up to the ceiling, then skimmed so low they had to duck.

"There it goes!" Chen shouted.

"Silence!" Ms McNicholas ordered.

In less than ten seconds, the whole class was back in their seats.

In a flash of grey and scarlet, the parrot soared upward, almost brushing the ceiling with its wings before settling on a raised blind that hung above the window nearest the front of the room.

"Don't make a sound," Ms McNicholas warned the class. She stretched out her arm towards the bird. "Come on," she murmured. "Don't be scared."

Everyone held their breath. Andi wished they could close the windows so the parrot couldn't fly out again, but any movement might frighten it away before they'd had time to close them all.

"Come on," Ms McNicholas urged. "We won't hurt you."

The parrot blinked a few times then spread its wings and fluttered down to her, its scarlet tail bobbing. It landed on her shoulder.

Ms McNicholas stroked the parrot's feathery chest. "There, now."

"She seems to know a bit about birds," Andi whispered to Nat.

"Hammer . . . slammer . . . aak," the parrot squawked.

The whole class laughed, including Ms McNicholas.

"Where did it come from?" Chen asked.

"And what are we going to do with it?" Tanya called. "Can we keep it?"

"What sort of bird is it?" asked someone behind Andi.

"Wait," Ms McNicholas said, holding up a hand. "I can't answer if you all call out at once."

Everyone stopped talking and waited.

"This is an African Grey," Ms McNicholas said. "And I don't know where it came from but we can't

keep it, that's certain. Tanya, will you go to the headteacher's office and ask her to call the RSPCA?"

Tanya sped out of the room.

"If you're sitting near an open window, shut it now so this little beauty can't fly away before the RSPCA officer arrives," Ms McNicholas continued.

The windows were slammed shut, making the parrot flap its wings in alarm. "It's OK," Ms McNicholas murmured to the bird.

The parrot settled down again as the teacher smoothed its feathers.

"What are we going to do with it until the RSPCA man comes?" said Howard.

"He can sit on my desk." Ms McNicholas emptied her heavy ceramic penholder to use as a perch.

The parrot looked at the pot with its head on one side, then hopped on to it, curling his claws over the rim.

"Perfect," Ms McNicholas said. "He'll be quite happy there while we get back to the Victorians."

"Aak!" the parrot squawked as the class returned to their studies.

Andi found it impossible to concentrate on the history lesson. The bird *had* to be lost – it wouldn't be flying around on its own otherwise. Andi felt a rush of excitement at the thought of another investigation for the PFC.

She studied the parrot as it perched on the edge of the penholder. Its feathers were in good condition, glossy and smooth, and its eyes were bright. It was clearly well cared for. *It doesn't look thin or hungry*, Andi thought, *so it can't have been missing for long*.

"Adam and Eve on a raft! Hammer slammer! Aak!" the parrot squawked.

"What is that bird talking about?" Natalie whispered.

Andi shrugged. She glanced at the clock, impatient for morning break to start. She couldn't wait to tell Tristan that the Pet Finders had a new case.

Unfortunately Ms McNicholas insisted that the class worked through morning break to make up for the time they'd lost over the parrot. When lunchtime came, Andi and Natalie raced out to the playground to find Tristan. He was talking to a group of friends.

"Tris, the Pet Finders have got a new case!" Natalie announced.

"An African Grey parrot flew into our classroom this morning," Andi explained.

"Wow! That's amazing!" Ella's voice sounded.

Natalie's smile faded as the new girl appeared from behind Tristan.

"Tell us everything," Ella demanded. "Where did it come from?"

"We don't know yet," Andi replied.

"We could try the zoo," Tristan suggested.

Natalie rummaged through her rucksack and pulled out her mobile phone. "I'll look up the number on the Internet and give them a ring."

"Don't bother. The zoo hasn't got any African Greys," Ella said. "I went there last weekend with my family."

Natalie frowned, but Tristan said, "Thanks, Ella. That's saved us a phone call."

Andi spotted Fisher coming out of the school

carrying a travel cage. To her surprise, the cage was empty. "There's Fisher," she said. "But where's the parrot?"

The Pet Finders and Ella pelted across the playground.

"Hi, kids," said Fisher.

"Aren't you taking the parrot?" Natalie asked.

"No. Nobody's reported a parrot missing, so Ms McNicholas offered to look after him for now. She used to keep exotic birds so she knows what she's doing. I'll bring a proper cage over for him later."

"She won't need to look after him for long," Ella said, "now that *we're* on the case!"

"Wait a sec!" Natalie exclaimed. "Who said *you* were in the Pet Finders Club, Ella?"

"Extra help will be useful," Tristan pointed out. "Let's go and have a look at the parrot. Perhaps we'll find a clue to tell us where it's come from."

"Oh, wait. I forgot. I've got to go to the library," Ella said. "I've got some really urgent homework, but I'll see you later, OK? I'll want to hear everything!"

"Do you want to be a Pet Finder or not?" Natalie queried, raising her eyebrows.

"Of course, but this can't wait. See you!" Ella ran off.

The Pet Finders crept back into Andi and Natalie's classroom and found the parrot walking back and forth along the edge of Ms McNicholas's desk. A few sunflower seeds were scattered on the tabletop and he stopped to eat one. "Aak! Adam and Eve on a raft! Aak!" he cried.

"Adam and Eve on a raft?" Tristan echoed. "What does *that* mean?"

"No idea," Natalie said with a shrug.

"Perhaps he rode on a raft to get to Aldcliffe," Andi suggested.

"Why would he use a raft when he can fly?" Tristan said.

"I wonder who Adam and Eve are?" Natalie said, shutting the door carefully so the parrot couldn't escape. "Two other birds, perhaps?"

"Or his owners," Andi said as the kids tiptoed towards the teacher's desk.

The parrot spread his wings and took off. He

completed a circuit of the room, then swooped low over Tristan's head and landed on the desk again. "Hot wax. Aak!"

"Hot sax?" Tristan said. "Perhaps his owner's a musician."

"It said *wax*." Natalie giggled. "Not sax. I wonder what it means."

Stroking the bird's soft feathery head with one finger, Andi studied him to see if he had any special markings or an ID tag. She noticed a small gold-coloured ring around its leg with a tiny gold palm tree attached.

"That's got to be a clue," Natalie said.

"It'll be a good security check, too," Tristan said. "If anyone phones to claim the parrot, we can ask what it wears on its leg. Parrots are pretty valuable; we don't want to give it to the wrong person."

"Good thinking," Andi told him.

"I'll take a picture for some lost-parrot posters," Natalie said, flipping her mobile phone open. As she snapped the photo, Ms McNicholas came in.

"What are you children doing in here?" she asked, surprised.

"We're the Pet Finders Club," Andi explained, "and we're looking for clues so we can track down the parrot's owner."

Ms McNicholas frowned. "What do you mean?"

Tristan whipped a flyer out of his rucksack and held it out to her. A black-and-white photo showed Andi, Tristan and Natalie standing in a row with their arms crossed and their faces determined. *Lost a Pet? Who Do You Need?* was printed across the top. At the bottom, in big bold letters, was written PET FINDERS!

"Hmm. I see," said Ms McNicholas. Her mouth twitched as if she was trying not to smile. "Very professional. I'm sure you'll be able to find Charlie's owner – but don't let the search interfere with your school work."

"Charlie?" Natalie said.

"I had a green-wing macaw called Charlie when I was a little girl. I thought I'd call this one the same until we find out his real name."

"You seem to know quite a lot about parrots," Andi said. "Can you tell us about their behaviour? Do they often fly away from home? And if they do,

47

will they try to find their way home again?"

"Greys are very cautious birds, and they're loyal to their owners. It's very rare for one to fly away."

"Well, this one has," Tristan pointed out. "And it's up to us to make sure he gets home again."

Chapter Five

The Pet Finders were still talking about the lost parrot as they headed for Clip 'n' Curl the next morning. "Charlie's owner must really miss him," Andi said. "The sooner we track down his owner the better."

They arrived at the grooming parlour at a few minutes to nine, just as Aggie was letting in the first customers of the day. She stopped to make a fuss of Jet and Buddy. "Hello, boys! Aren't you adorable?"

Buddy and Jet wagged their tails in agreement.

Inside the salon, Joe and Lena were already at their stations, laying out brushes for their first clients.

Joe waved. "Have you brought in Buddy and Jet to be groomed?"

Buddy jerked back on his lead and Andi laughed. "It's OK, boy," she said. "You're not going to be groomed today."

Jet hid behind Tristan and Natalie, trying – and failing – to make himself look small.

"I thought Buddy liked being bathed," Natalie said as Tristan helped her heave Jet inside.

Andi picked up Buddy and carried him through the door. "He does, usually. Perhaps he doesn't like the look of all those brushes."

"Or more likely he saw the costumes!" Tristan joked.

"Why don't you put the two of them out in the kennels?" Aggie suggested.

Once they were through the salon, the dogs relaxed. They trotted into the kennel area, a wide sunny room with patio doors that looked out over the back garden. A stack of glittery deluxe pet-carriers in an assortment of colours was piled against the far wall. There were four pens in the kennels, all of them large enough to hold two dogs, and each contained a comfortable doggy quilt, a water bowl, and a few toys.

They placed the dogs in the sunniest pen next to the window. Jet settled down on the cosy quilt, perfectly happy, and Buddy snuggled up beside him.

"Let's go dog-washing," Andi said.

The Pet Finders headed back to the salon and put on plastic aprons.

A moment later the door opened and David Nazrallah walked in carrying a glittery pink dog-carrier and a matching holdall. "Hello," he said. "I didn't know you helped out here."

"We've just started," Tristan told him.

David opened the holdall. "I've brought everything Honey will need. Herbal shampoo, some of her favourite snacks and her towel." He laid them on Aggie's workstation.

Andi ran a warm bath, adding a generous squirt of Honey's shampoo. When the water was ready, she lifted Honey in and began to wash her, working the lather right down to her skin as Aggie had shown her.

"I shouldn't think you'll need any help here," Natalie said. "Honey's so small you could wash her

51

one-handed. I'll go and see who's next for grooming."

Lena led a bearded collie over from the waiting area. "Tristan, could you help me hold Digby, please? He's only come in for an eyebrow trim but he can never sit still when I've got clippers in my hand."

Tristan helped her lift the shaggy dog on to her worktable.

"We'll have to get going on the parrot posters soon, Andi," Tristan reminded her over Digby's head.

"They're done," Andi said. "Nat emailed me the picture last night and I printed the posters off this morning."

"Good work!" said Tristan.

"I can't stop thinking about that palm tree charm," Andi went on. "I'm sure Nat's right about it being a clue. But what does it mean? Perhaps Charlie's owner comes from the West Indies."

"Or perhaps his owner's mad about coconuts," Tristan offered.

When Honey was clean, Andi pulled out the

bath plug and switched on the shower. With a high-pitched yap, Honey scampered into the spray of warm water. She spun round in a circle, shaking droplets all over Andi.

Laughing, Andi rinsed off the last of the lather, switched off the shower and grabbed Honey's fluffy towel. The little chihuahua seized the corner of the towel in her teeth and yanked it playfully. *Honey might be a champion show-dog, but she knows how to play just as well as any pet*, Andi thought, pleased.

She wrapped Honey in the towel and carried her across to Aggie's grooming table. She rubbed Honey gently, then unwrapped her. The little dog's damp hair stood out in tan hedgehog spikes.

Natalie came back from the waiting area with a cute tan-and-white cocker spaniel. "He's got some burrs tangled in his coat, Joe. His owner hoped you could get them out without giving him a haircut," she said, handing him the lead. "Oh, doesn't Honey look sweet," she went on, catching sight of the chihuahua. "Can we style her hair for you, Aggie?"

"After I've clipped her," Aggie said. "If that's all right with you, David."

"That's fine," David replied. "I'm sure you'll make her look lovely."

"Would she like to wear one of the costumes?" Natalie asked hopefully.

"No thanks," David said. "I think she'll be happier with a nice pink bow to match her carrier and towel."

Tristan came over. The bearded collie's eyebrows had been trimmed and he was sitting happily while Lena brushed his long fur.

"How's Ella, Tris?" Andi asked, grabbing a broom to sweep up fallen hair from the floor.

Tristan looked puzzled. "OK, I suppose. Or at least she was yesterday, at school."

"So, have you asked her out on a *date* yet?" Natalie said meaningfully, stopping on her way across the salon with an armful of clean towels.

Tristan blushed. "No!"

"I think you've got a crush on her, Tris," Andi teased.

Tristan's face turned redder than ever. "I haven't!"

"You're right, Andi," Natalie agreed. "Anyone can see it." She gave Andi an exaggerated wink.

Tristan snatched the broom from Andi and began sweeping under Joe's workstation. "We should be talking about the parrot," he said. "Let's go to the Banana Beach Café when we've finished here. Maggie and Jango know about parrots because they've got Long John Silver, so perhaps they can give us some hints to help us find Charlie's owner."

"Good idea," Andi said.

"I phoned the zoo," Natalie said, "even though Ella said not to bother."

"Have they lost an African Grey?" Andi asked.

"No, Ella was right. They haven't got any African Greys."

"And Charlie isn't from Paws for Thought or Christine would have told us," Andi said, thinking out loud. "So he must be someone's pet."

"Someone who likes palm trees," Tristan said. He swept a pile of hair into a dustpan and deposited it in the bin.

"Honey's ready, girls," Aggie called. She'd brushed the chihuahua's fur, leaving it smooth and shiny. "She's still a bit damp in places," she added, "so you could finish her off with the hairdryer."

Natalie fetched the brush Aggie had been using on Honey – a soft-bristle one – and Andi plugged in the hairdryer.

Honey stood patiently while they brushed her hair this way and that as they decided which style suited her best. Just as Andi directed the hairdryer on to Honey's chest a tall woman carrying a white pet-carrier burst through the salon door. A tiny black-and-white dog peeped out through the carrier's grille.

"Hello, Amanda," Aggie greeted the woman. "I'm not quite ready for you. Would you mind taking Windwhistle into the waiting area?"

"Actually, I would. You know he hates waiting." The woman let her gaze fall on Andi and Natalie. "New staff, I see," she said. "I'm Mrs Slinger and this –" she opened the pet-carrier and lifted out her dog, another long-haired chihuahua "this is Windwhistle. Take a good look because he is going to be the champion of the Aldcliffe Pet Show!"

"Now, Amanda," David said, sliding off the chrome stool where he'd been watching Honey have her grooming session. "There are plenty of other dogs in the competition. Anyone could win it – including Honey." He was smiling but Andi could see that he was annoyed by Amanda Slinger's boast.

"Don't be so sure, David. Lydia Baxter is judging the miniature dogs," said Mrs Slinger. "And she has spoken very highly of Windwhistle." She held the chihuahua close to her face. "Isn't that right, precious? My little poppet's going to win first prize, isn't he?"

Windwhistle's tiny tail began to wag.

"There, he knows who's the champion," Mrs Slinger cooed.

"We'll see," David said.

Andi and Natalie finished styling Honey's fur and stood back to admire her. Her golden-and-white fur was smooth on her body but they'd fluffed it out around her head like a lion's mane. Natalie had sprayed on a little non-scented hairspray to keep it in place. Andi cut off a length of pink ribbon and tied it round Honey's neck before presenting her to David.

"She looks beautiful," he declared. "You've done a wonderful job, girls."

"Thanks!" said Natalie. "Honey is so sweet and pretty, I'm sure she'll be good competition for Windwhistle," she added loyally.

That got Andi thinking. What if all the dogs at the Aldcliffe Pet Show were this well-bred and pampered? Would scruffy, lovable Bud stand a chance of winning a prize at all?

"I love helping out at the grooming parlour," Andi announced as the Pet Finders headed for the Banana Beach Café at lunchtime.

"Aggie seems pretty happy about it too," Natalie said.

They reached the café and Andi and Tristan went inside, leaving Natalie outside with Buddy and Jet.

"Hey, where have you been?" Maggie Pearce greeted them, wiping her hands on her bright floral apron. "Jango and I haven't seen you for ages."

"We're back at school now," Tristan said, "but we're working on a new pet-finding case – or actually, an *owner*-finding case."

"We've found a parrot," Andi added. "We thought you might be able to help us."

Long John Silver, Maggie and Jango's beautiful blue-and-green parrot, fluttered down on to the counter. "More bananas!" he squawked.

"We'll be glad to help if we can," Maggie said. "Do you want anything to eat or drink? We're doing delicious chicken wraps today."

"Yes, please," Andi said. "And we'll all have Banana Spice smoothies."

"Sit yourselves down," Maggie said, "and I'll bring them out to you. Then Jango and I will have time to chat."

Andi and Tristan joined Natalie outside at a table that was shaded by a rainbow-striped sun umbrella. Buddy jumped up, planting his paws on Andi's knee.

Andi patted him, then delved into her rucksack and pulled out a stack of pink paper. "Here. I made these last night."

HAVE YOU LOST A PARROT? was written at the top in bold letters. Below was the photo Natalie had taken, showing Charlie on Ms McNicholas's desk. The picture was rather fuzzy but it still showed the parrot's grey plumage and scarlet tail. Andi's phone number was printed at the bottom of the poster.

"Great," said Tristan. "Hopefully this will get us a few leads." He pointed at the blurry photo. "Looks like you need a new phone, Nat."

"My phone's top of the range," Natalie retorted. "And at least I've *got* a mobile, not like *some* people I know."

"I have got a phone," Tristan said.

"It's broken," Natalie reminded him. "Which is why you shouldn't go skateboarding with it in your pocket."

"Stop it, you two," Andi said, jumping in to halt the argument. "We've got to focus on the case."

Jango Pearce, Maggie's husband, came out of the café carrying three plates. A yellow apron strained across his large stomach and his greying hair stood on end, as if he had been running his hands through it. "Did I hear that you're looking for a lost parrot?" he asked, setting their plates down on the table.

"No, we've found a parrot and need to track down the owner," Natalie corrected him. "You haven't heard of anyone who's lost an African Grey, have you, Jango?"

He shook his head. "Sorry. But I'll put up a poster for you."

"This bird is a real talker," Andi said. Another thought struck her. "Hey, perhaps it could tell us its address."

Jango laughed. "Parrots don't really talk. They just copy what they hear. Take Long John Silver, for instance: he says 'more bananas' because he hears Maggie say that all day."

Maggie brought out the smoothies. "My aunt had a parrot," she said, sitting in the empty chair at their table. "It used to make barking noises because her neighbour's dog barked non-stop."

"And my musician friend's parrot, he sounds just like a guitar," Jango added.

Natalie groaned. "So all that stuff Charlie says doesn't mean anything. It's useless."

"No, it's not!" Andi exclaimed, almost choking on her chicken wrap. "It could still be a really important clue!" She pulled a scrap of paper out of her pocket. "Quick, let's write down everything he says!"

Maggie handed her a pen.

"He says, 'Adam and Eve on a raft' a lot," Natalie said.

Andi scribbled it down.

"And 'hammer slammer' and 'hot wax'," Tristan added. "But how could that be important? It's just gibberish."

"Don't you see?" Andi said. "All we have to work out is where he learnt those words and we'll have cracked the case!"

Chapter Six

Next morning the Pet Finders met up at half past nine to put up the posters about the parrot.

"Let's put one in Rachel's shop," Tristan suggested. A friendly woman called Rachel Brand ran a corner shop not far from Andi's house and she was always willing to display a pet-finding poster.

As they reached the shop, Ms McNicholas came out carrying a newspaper. "Hello," she said. "Any luck with finding Charlie's owner?"

"Not yet," Andi replied. "But we've made some posters." She handed one to the teacher.

"This is terrific," Ms McNicholas said. "It looks as though it won't be long before I lose my new feathered friend." She smiled, but Andi wondered if the teacher was hoping they wouldn't find the parrot's owner too soon. "I've brought him home for the weekend," Ms McNicholas went on. "Would you like to visit him?"

"You bet!" the Pet Finders cried.

"I'll just take this poster inside," Tristan said. He darted into the shop. A minute later he was out again. "Rachel's going to put it up for us."

"Great!" Andi said.

It took only a few minutes to walk to Ms McNicholas's flat, which was in a small block not far from Andi's house. "Up here," the teacher said, leading the way to the second floor and unlocking a blue front door.

Half-filled boxes were everywhere and the living-room table was covered in rolls of pale-green wallpaper and tins of paint. Beside them, a small box of nails and a hammer were spilling out of a bag from the local DIY shop. "As you can see, I'm still settling in," Ms McNicholas said.

Charlie sat on the perch in a large cage by the window, looking very much at home.

"I'll let him out," Ms McNicholas said. "He could

do with stretching his wings." She opened the cage door.

Charlie hopped down to the doorway and peeked outside the cage before spreading his wings and flying across the room. "Adam and Eve on a raft!" he squawked as he landed on the table beside the rolls of wallpaper.

"Cool wallpaper," Tristan said.

"Thanks," Ms McNicholas said. "I'm having it in here with matching green paint on the door and window frames."

"Paint it red!" Charlie squawked, flying to the curtain pole. "Short lumberjack!"

Andi laughed. "Where could Charlie have heard these weird phrases?"

"Maybe 'paint it red' is a comment on my home improvements," Ms McNicholas joked. "Perhaps he's not keen on green."

"Perhaps he belongs to a decorator or a lumberjack," Tristan suggested. Then he frowned. "Do you get lumberjacks in England? I thought they came from America or Canada or somewhere."

"Perhaps his owner is *from* America or Canada but

67

he or she lives here now," Andi said thoughtfully.

"Hammer slammer!" shrieked Charlie. "Hammer slammer! Short lumberjack!"

Natalie gave a squeal. "Of course! Decorators use paint, lumberjacks deal in timber, and carpenters use hammers. I bet he came from a DIY shop!"

"Brilliant, Nat!" Andi exclaimed, patting Natalie on the back. "And there's no reason why someone who works at the DIY shop shouldn't be an American, is there?"

"But where do Adam and Eve come in?" Tristan asked.

"Charlie might have heard that from someone else," Natalie said. "Anyway, it's got to be worth going to a DIY shop and asking if any of the staff has lost a parrot."

"The Do It Yourself Depot is the one closest to the school," Tristan said. "We should start there."

"We can go straight away," Ms McNicholas said. "I forgot to buy any wallpaper paste." She stretched her arm out to Charlie and the parrot flew down, landing on her wrist. "Let's put you back in your cage, boy," she said, stroking his feathery head.

"Paint it red! Paint it red!" Charlie squawked as Ms McNicholas carried him to the cage.

The teacher laughed. "Sorry, Charlie, no can do. This room's going to be green, and that's that!"

Ms McNicholas's car was parked in the parking area behind the flats. "Wow!" Tristan gasped, impressed. It was a shiny red MG, with cream leather seats and a huge, narrow steering wheel.

"What a fantastic car!" Tristan whistled.

Ms McNicholas smiled. "Thanks. My father spent ten years restoring it and gave it to me when I left university. I have to say, it's one of the things I love most in the world!" She opened the passenger door. "The only downside is that it's a long way from being a minivan! I'm afraid two of you will have to squash in the back."

"I'm in front!" Tristan said quickly.

Andi and Natalie clambered into the back of the car. There was hardly any room for them and they had to sit with their knees almost up to their chins. Not that Andi minded being a bit uncomfortable – not when they might be about to solve a case.

"This car is so cool," Tristan said, settling himself in the front seat. He ran his fingers over the cream dashboard. "I want one exactly the same when I'm old enough to drive."

"I'm not having a lift in it, then," Natalie said. "Not if I have to sit in the back."

"I don't remember offering you one," Tristan replied.

It took about five minutes to reach the Do It Yourself Depot, a large warehouse-like building set in a huge car park. Ms McNicholas parked beside a white van and they all piled out.

Inside, the shop was packed, but to Andi's delight she spotted a rack of promising books beside the door. "Look at these," she said, scanning the titles. *"How to Build a Cage for Your Bird, Decorating for Bird-Lovers, Tropical Décor* . . . it looks as though a bird-lover chose to sell these books!"

They hurried to the customer-service desk to ask if any of the staff owned a parrot, while Ms McNicholas went off to find wallpaper paste.

"A parrot? I can't stand birds," the saleswoman said with a shudder. "All that fluttering!"

"But do you know anyone on the staff who owns one?" Andi prompted her.

The woman frowned. "No, I don't think anyone's got a parrot."

"What about all the decorating books for bird-lovers?" Tristan said, pointing to the rack

"Some of our customers buy them," the woman said with a shrug. "That's why we sell them."

"It looks like a dead end," Natalie sighed as they left the desk, but the cashier called them back.

"Hang on, I think Harry might have some birds. He works in the timber section at the back of the shop."

"Timber," Tristan whispered. "That could tie in with our lumberjack clue!"

They raced to the back of the shop and found an older man in a brown overall unloading a trolley-load of planks. "Do you think that's him?" Andi said quietly.

"Let's go and find out," Tristan replied.

They stepped forward. "Excuse me, are you Harry?" Natalie asked.

The man turned and ran a hand through his

wispy grey hair. "Yes. Can I help you?"

"The cashier said you keep birds. We've found a lost parrot." Tristan pulled a poster out of his rucksack. "We thought it might be yours."

Harry waved the poster away. "Sorry, son. I've got a few canaries – but no parrots."

Andi's heart sank. The trail had gone cold again.

Ms McNicholas was waiting for them at the front of the shop. "No luck?" she guessed when she spotted their gloomy faces. "I suppose it was a bit of a long shot."

As they went out of the shop, a breeze sprang up and blew across the car park. Andi watched an empty cola can rattle across the tarmac.

That was when she saw it – their biggest clue yet!

Chapter Seven

"Look at that!" Andi cried as a bright-red feather skittered across the ground. "It's just like the ones in Charlie's tail! Perhaps he comes from a house near here." She sprinted after the feather and caught it as it whirled into the air. Holding it tight, she darted back across the car park.

"Where did it come from?" Natalie asked.

"Which direction is the wind blowing?" Tristan licked his index finger and raised it in the air, but it was impossible to tell.

"Please can we scout around and see if we can find out where the feather's come from, Ms McNicholas?" Natalie said.

Ms McNicholas frowned. "Well, I don't know . . ."

"Don't worry. We do this sort of thing all the time when we're looking for pets," Tristan said. "We won't take very long."

"OK. I'll wait in the car. Good luck!"

Andi jogged across the car park with Tristan and Natalie close behind her. To the right of the Do It Yourself Depot was a car showrooms. It was closed so the Pet Finders peered in through the big windows. There was no empty parrot cage inside. "I don't think he came from here," Tristan said.

To the left of the DIY shop was a community centre, a modern red-brick building with a green roof. "Do community centres have parrots?" Andi asked doubtfully.

"There's only one way to find out," Natalie said.

They headed towards it, through a small garden full of wind-tossed flowers. Suddenly the door opened and lots of well-dressed people streamed out, led by a photographer with an expensive-looking camera slung around his neck. "Let's have you in a big group on the steps," he said, throwing his arms wide. "That's it. Smaller people in front, tall ones behind."

The Pet Finders hesitated. They could hardly push through the crowd to get to the front door when the people were having pictures taken.

"Oh no!" Andi said, catching sight of a woman in the centre of the group. She was wearing a spectacular hat decorated with red feathers.

Natalie groaned. "I bet the feather we found came from her hat."

"She could still be Charlie's owner," Tristan pointed out. "She might save Charlie's old feathers to decorate her hats."

"Let's go and ask," Andi suggested as the photographer snapped the group shot.

"Excuse me," Natalie said to the woman in the feathery hat. "Do you own a parrot?"

"No." The woman shook her head, setting the feathers fluttering. She smiled suddenly. "Oh, you mean the hat! I didn't make it. I bought it in town."

"Oh," Andi said, disappointed again. "Thanks."

The Pet Finders headed back to Ms McNicholas's car. "Those feathers were too bright anyway," Natalie admitted.

"And if all of them had come out of Charlie's tail, he'd be bald!" Tristan added.

Andi couldn't help laughing. "We'll just have to work with the clues we've got – all those weird things Charlie says and the palm tree charm round his leg."

"The trouble is, none of them makes any sense," Natalie pointed out. "It's almost as frustrating as having no clues at all!"

Andi spent so much time at the weekend trying to solve the lost parrot case that she hardly had a moment with Buddy. She raced home from school on Monday to work on his trick for the pet show. "Today's the day we're going to get this right, Bud," she said, taking the hoop into the back garden.

Buddy watched her with his head on one side.

"Come on, boy. Through you go."

The little terrier scampered up to the hoop, then flopped down on the grass beside it.

"You've got to go *through* it." Andi took a dog treat out of her pocket and tossed it through the hoop. "Go on, boy!"

Buddy ran round the side of the hoop and wolfed down the treat.

"Oh, Buddy," Andi groaned.

Natalie appeared at the back door with Jet. "Hello, Andi. Your mum said you were out here. How's it going?"

Andi shrugged. "It's not."

Buddy ran off down the yard to play with his rubber bone. Jet loped after him.

"I don't know what to do next," Andi admitted. "I've tried throwing treats through the hoop, but he just nips round the side to gobble them up."

"Why don't you *show* him how it's done?" Natalie suggested. "Here, I'll hold the hoop and you jump through it."

Andi handed the hoop to Natalie, then called Buddy. He trotted over, his tail wagging. Jet followed and settled down in a patch of sunshine.

"Come on, Bud. Pay attention," Andi commanded. She ran to the hoop, crouched down, then hopped through awkwardly and glanced back to see what Buddy was doing.

He was watching her with his tongue hanging out.

"Come on, boy." Andi caught his collar and led him to the hoop. She jumped through again, pulling Buddy after her. "See? That's what you have to do!"

Letting go of his collar, Andi jumped through the hoop once more. To her delight, Buddy copied her. "He did it! Good boy, Bud! Good boy!" She hugged him. "Now, let's see you go through by yourself."

Buddy scurried round the hoop and jumped through.

"Yes!" Andi cried. "This calls for a celebration dog treat." She felt inside the pockets of her red hoodie. "Oops! I've used up all his treats."

"Let's go to Paws for Thought and buy some," Natalie suggested. "We can give the dogs a run in the park on the way."

The pet shop was packed with people. "Look, there's Belle," Andi said, recognizing a beautiful white husky that she'd bathed at Aggie's grooming parlour. She ran her hands through the dog's soft fluffy coat and Belle cuddled her head against Andi's jeans.

Natalie stretched up on tiptoe. "Where's Tris? I thought he was supposed to be helping Christine today."

Andi scanned the shop. She could just make out a mop of red hair underneath a sign saying PET SHOW ENTRY FORMS. "There he is."

They wove their way through the crowd, admiring the well-groomed dogs they passed. Tristan was standing at a table on the far side of the shop, handing out entry forms for the pet show.

"Thank goodness! Can you give me a hand?" He thrust a pile of forms at Andi. "Everyone wants to register for the pet show and I can't give these forms out fast enough."

Andi and Natalie helped to hand out the forms and gradually the pet-owners moved away from the table. Even so, the rest of the shop was still crowded. There were at least a dozen people queuing up at the till.

When Christine had finally finished ringing everything up, she came over to speak to them. "Wow! That was a rush. Poor Max is hiding out the back."

"You and Fisher are doing an amazing job of organizing this show," Natalie said. "So many people are entering their pets."

"It's been great for business," Christine said. "And not only for my shop. The hotels are booked all the way into Lancaster and restaurant reservations are soaring too." She turned to Tristan. "I've got another job for you, if you're up for it."

"'Course he is," Natalie replied. "Tristan likes hard work, don't you, Tris?"

Tristan gave her a fake scowl. "Thanks."

"Come on," Christine said. She led the kids into the stockroom. Two boxes brimming with papers sat on a low shelf. "These are all the pet show applications that came in the post. We've got to send everyone a programme. OK?"

"Yep." Tristan picked up one of the boxes. "We'll do it at the table in the shop in case anyone else comes in for an entry form."

"*We?*" Natalie teased. "I don't remember volunteering to help you, Tris."

Tristan stared at her in dismay. "Come on, Nat. It'll take me for ever to do it all by myself."

Andi laughed. "She's only joking. Of course we'll help." She grabbed a pile of printed sheets and followed Tristan back to the table.

"Hey, here comes Amanda Slinger," Natalie said, as they sat at the table in the shop. "I wonder if she's brought Windwhistle with her."

Mrs Slinger entered the shop. Her little chihuahua was in his pet-carrier, peeping out through the grille. She set the box down, opened the door and lifted Windwhistle out, putting him on the floor beside her. "You stretch your legs, darling. But stay close to me." She headed for the table where the Pet Finders were sitting.

"Well, you're very busy," she commented. "Do you work at Clip 'n' Curl *and* Paws for Thought?"

"We're helping out today because—" Tristan started.

Mrs Slinger didn't let him finish. "Has

82

Windwhistle's herbal food supplement arrived yet?"

"Sorry, I don't know," Tristan said. "Christine deals with special orders."

Christine came out of the storeroom. "It's not in yet, I'm afraid, Amanda."

Andi noticed Buddy watching Windwhistle with interest as the tiny dog sniffed around the table. Buddy trotted over to make friends, but when he sniffed Windwhistle, the chihuahua gave a frightened yelp and dived into his pet-carrier.

Buddy stared at him for a minute then flopped down beside Andi.

"Did the big dog scare you, my precious?" Mrs Slinger crooned. Windwhistle peered up at her, looking very anxious. She snapped the carrier shut and picked it up. "Don't worry. We're going home now," she said, and marched out of the shop.

"Poor Windwhistle," Andi said. "Buddy must have looked like a giant to him. But wasn't he sweet, peeping out of his carrier?"

"I don't think there's anything sweet about a dog that has to be carried around in an oversized handbag!" Tristan exclaimed. "Why doesn't he walk, like every other dog?"

"Probably because he's so tiny," Andi said. "I should think everything must seem scary when you're no bigger than a slipper." She patted Buddy. "Though I can't imagine why he was afraid of you, Bud. You wouldn't hurt a fly."

Buddy licked her hand, then turned his head to inspect the shop.

"He's searching for a fly so he can prove you wrong," Tristan joked. "Now come on, let's start sending out these programmes or we'll be here all night."

That evening, Andi's mum came home late from work. "What a day!" Mrs Talbot sank into an armchair. She took off her glasses and rubbed the bridge of her nose, then fluffed her short curly hair with both hands. "I didn't stop once."

"Can I help with dinner?" Andi offered. She and her mum lived on their own; Andi's parents had divorced a while ago, and her dad lived in Arizona where he worked as an oil-plant engineer. Luckily her parents were still good friends and she got to see her dad during the school holidays. Occasionally he came over to England on business, too, and he always managed to fit in a visit to Aldcliffe.

"Actually, I thought we'd go out tonight. We've both been so busy lately, it'd be nice to have a bit of girl-time, don't you think?"

Andi ran up to her room and dressed in her favourite lilac top and a pair of black jeans with a sequinned purple belt. Her mum was waiting in the hall when she ran downstairs and Buddy was sitting by the door, eyeing his lead hopefully. "Sorry. You can't come with us, Bud," Andi said, rubbing his chest. She hated to leave him alone. "We'll try and bring you back a doggy bag, OK?"

Andi's mum took her to a nearby café, which was warm, bright, and bustling. A waitress, who wore her greying hair in a stiff, old-fashioned beehive, showed them to a table near the counter. She handed them menus, then waited while they chose.

"I'll have hamburger and chips, please," Andi told her. "What are you having, Mum?"

"I'm not sure. I don't want anything too filling. In fact, what I'm really in the mood for is some breakfast."

"Breakfast at night?"

Mrs Talbot laughed. "Call me mad."

"OK," Andi said. "You're mad, Mum!"

"All-day breakfasts are at the bottom of the menu," the waitress said, pointing to the list.

Mrs Talbot scanned it quickly. "Two eggs on toast, please," she said.

"I think I'll have breakfast, too," Andi said, checking the menu again. "I'd like a bacon sandwich. With ketchup."

The waitress jotted the order in her notepad and walked away.

"You seem to be doing a good job with Buddy's training," said Mrs Talbot.

"Thanks," Andi said. "I finally got him to jump through the hoop but it took a lot of treats to get there."

"How's the parrot case going?"

"Well, we've put up posters and we've got loads of clues but—" Andi stopped abruptly as she heard the waitress call their order to the cook in the kitchen.

"A hammer slammer and paint it red! Adam and Eve on a raft!"

Chapter Eight

Hammer slammer! Paint it red! Adam and Eve on a raft! Andi almost fell off her chair. It was exactly what Charlie had been saying! Andi waved to the waitress. "Excuse me!"

The woman bustled back to their table. "Have you changed your mind again, dear?" she asked.

"No, but I heard you say 'Adam and Eve on a raft'," Andi said. "What does it mean?"

The waitress laughed. "Oh, it's just a fun way to say two eggs on toast. When I was young we had lots of nicknames for orders."

"What's a 'hammer slammer'?" Andi asked.

"A bacon sandwich," the woman told her. " 'Paint it red' means with tomato ketchup, of course."

"You haven't lost a parrot, have you?" Andi asked, her hopes soaring.

The waitress stared at Andi as though she had two heads. "A parrot? Uh, no."

"What about anyone else who works here?" Andi persisted.

The waitress shook her head. "Sorry." A man at the far end of the café raised his hand to attract her attention. "I've got to go." She hurried away.

Andi's mum raised her eyebrows. "What was all that about?"

"Charlie keeps saying these weird things," Andi explained. "Like 'Adam and Eve on a raft', and 'paint it red'. Parrots repeat things they hear, so now there must be a good chance our lost parrot comes from a café."

"I'm impressed," Mrs Talbot remarked. "It takes a lot of brains to work out such a tricky clue."

"Thanks, Mum," Andi said. "Now all I've got to do is phone all the cafés in Aldcliffe and find out which one's lost a parrot."

Mrs Talbot smiled. "I think that'll have to wait until tomorrow. Here comes our dinner."

Andi turned to see the waitress heading their way with a tray of eggs and bacon. "Don't you mean *breakfast?*" she corrected with a grin.

Andi could hardly wait for lunchtime next day. Ms McNicholas had given the Pet Finders permission to borrow the Yellow Pages so they could phone the Aldcliffe cafés and track down Charlie's owner.

Andi perched on a table in the classroom and flipped the directory to the right page. "There are loads of cafés and restaurants in the Lancaster area, but only about ten in Aldcliffe. We'll start with those and cross our fingers that Charlie didn't fly any further, otherwise we could be phoning for the rest of our lives!"

"Another case almost solved!" Tristan cheered. "Thank goodness your mum took you out for a meal last night!"

"I should have realized Charlie was talking in café slang," Ella said. "My aunt in London used to live next door to a café and she always calls coffee 'Joe' because that's the slang name for it."

"Everyone knows *that* one," Natalie said irritably, but Ella was still talking.

"My mum and dad took me to a café once that had the most amazing doughnuts," she went on. "They were shaped like stars and they came in every flavour you could possibly think of. Raspberry, vanilla, cinnamon, blueberry—"

"Ella, we've got to phone these cafés." Andi was afraid Ella's list of flavours might take up the whole lunch break.

"Oh yeah. I wish I'd brought my mobile to school today. It's the latest model and—"

"You read out the numbers, Tris," Natalie said, ignoring Ella, "Andi and I will make the calls."

"I don't mind phoning some of the cafés if someone will lend me their phone," Ella offered.

"No thanks," Natalie snapped.

Tristan read out the first number on the list and Andi punched it into her phone. While it was ringing, Natalie dialled the number of the second café on the list.

A man answered Andi's call: "The Light Bite."

"Hello," Andi said. "My friends and I have found a parrot. Have you lost one?"

"Pardon?"

"A parrot," she repeated. "It knows café slang so we thought it must come from a café."

"What is this? A prank phone call? Shouldn't you be at school?"

"No! Wait! I'm—" Andi tried to explain, but the man hung up. "Um, I don't think Charlie comes from the Light Bite," she told the others.

"No one's lost a parrot at the café in Mill Road either," Natalie said.

Andi punched in a new number, hoping to get a better response.

But to their disappointment, none of the Aldcliffe cafés and restaurants had lost a parrot.

"That's that, then," Andi said, snapping her phone shut after she'd called the last place on the list. "Now what?"

"I've got a horrible feeling we're going to have to ring every café and restaurant in Lancaster," Tristan said. He flipped over page after page of café listings. "Twenty-three pages. It's going to take for ever."

"But Charlie didn't seem tired when he flew through our classroom window," Natalie pointed out. "Surely he'd have been worn out if he'd flown all the way from Lancaster?"

"Well, perhaps he stopped to rest on the way," said Tristan.

"Why don't we photocopy these pages and divide them up?" Ella suggested. "Then we can phone from home."

"Or *three* of us can, anyway," Natalie muttered. "This is the Pet Finders' case, after all."

Ella didn't seem to hear. "I'll go and ask Ms McNicholas if we can use the photocopier in the school office."

"I'll come with you." Tristan followed her out of the room.

Andi went to the window and gazed out. It was hard to stay focused when all their clues seemed to lead nowhere. Minutes ago she'd thought they were close to solving the case, but now it felt as though they were as far away from finding Charlie's owner as ever.

* * *

After an hour of phoning cafés after school, Andi was glad to help at Clip 'n' Curl. It was crammed with customers when she arrived and the phone was ringing non-stop. The waiting area had overflowed and people were standing in the salon with dogs of all shapes and sizes. There were even a few clients with cats, who were eyeing the dogs nervously from inside their carriers.

"I am *so* glad to see you!" Aggie greeted her. "Natalie's just taken a beagle down to the kennels. Tristan hasn't arrived yet, but I'm sure he'll be here in a minute. Would you run the bath, please, and start washing Spot? He's in the waiting room. Some of these people are waiting to pay so I need to deal with them first."

"OK." Andi went to the bath and turned on the taps.

Joe was trying to groom a wriggling tan dachshund and Honey was sitting on Lena's table, having her nails clipped. Andi went over to stroke her. "I didn't expect to see her back so soon," she said, running her hand gently over Honey's fluffy head. "She was only here the other day."

"David thought her nails were getting a tiny bit too long and there won't be time to clip them on Saturday when she comes for her final wash and brush-up before the show," Lena explained.

Andi went back to check the water level in the bath. As she squirted in a dollop of shampoo, she heard the door open and wondered if it was Tristan.

Mrs Slinger entered with Windwhistle in his pet-carrier. "I need a new collar and lead for the show, Aggie," she called. "Be a dear and find me your very best, will you?"

"In a moment," Aggie replied. "When I've finished with the customers who are waiting."

Tristan arrived. "Did you have any luck ringing cafés?" he asked Andi, swishing the bath water with his hand to make it more bubbly.

"No. I'm going to try again . . ." She trailed off, realizing that Tristan was no longer listening. He was staring across the room, his face pink with excitement.

"Look at that, Andi," he hissed, nodding to the other side of the salon. "That woman at the till has got parrot badges all over her hat! *And* she's holding a pack of bird food with a picture of an African Grey on it. She could be Charlie's owner!"

The woman finished paying and walked out of the door with her beautifully-groomed Pekingese trotting beside her.

Tristan raced towards the door. "Wait!" As he ran, a red setter on an extendable lead bounded in front of him. The lead pulled taut and Tristan tripped over it, crashing on to the floor and knocking over a display of fancy collars.

Pandemonium broke out. Dogs began barking and pulling on their leads. Some broke free and began to tear through the salon, swerving round anyone who got in their way. Big dogs leapt over smaller ones. Leads tangled. Owners yelled their dogs' names, trying to get them under control. Cats, still safely in their carriers, hissed and wailed furiously, adding to the din.

Andi quickly turned off the bath taps and ran to help Tristan, but she couldn't get through the chaos. She noticed a man with a dachshund enter the salon, gasp at the scene and quickly exit, leaving the front door wide open.

Oh, no. A dog might get out! Andi thought, worried. She called to a man with a quivering Yorkie who had taken cover behind the front counter. "Shut the door, please!" she cried. But he didn't move, too busy trying to calm his terrified dog.

A German Shepherd raced past Andi. She caught its lead and held on tight. "Who owns this one?" she shouted.

A woman grabbed the lead from her. "He's mine. Thanks."

Finally Andi reached Tristan, who was now on his feet. "Are you OK?" she asked.

"Nothing broken," he said, giving Andi an embarrassed grin. "But look what I've done."

"Don't worry about it," Andi said. "Let's catch these dogs quick and give them back to their owners." She set off after a Great Dane.

Natalie came running in from the kennels and caught a yapping terrier by its collar. Aggie, Joe and Lena joined in grabbing dogs, too. Before long, all the pets were rounded up and handed over to their owners.

"I'm really sorry, Aggie," Tristan apologized after

he handed a half-brushed dachshund back to Joe.

"It was an accident. And no real harm's been done." Aggie righted a fallen laundry bin and stuffed the spilt wet towels back inside it.

Andi picked up a pin brush from the floor and rewound a reel of tangled ribbon.

"I'll go and fetch the next dog," Natalie said. As she headed for the waiting area, David Nazrallah came into the shop.

"Hello, is Honey ready?"

Andi glanced around, wondering who was looking after the tiny dog. In all the confusion, she hadn't even noticed her. But Aggie, Joe and Lena were looking round as if they didn't know where Honey was either, and she wasn't being held by anyone in the crowd of customers.

Andi thought hard. She had last seen Honey perched on Lena's worktable having her nails clipped. Perhaps she was hiding somewhere nearby. Trying to stay calm, she bent down and scanned the floor in all directions. There was no sign of her.

"What's up?" said David.

"Come out the back, David," Aggie said, her face

taut with anxiety. She led him through the purple velvet curtain.

"We've got to find Honey," Andi whispered to her friends.

They searched under tables, in laundry bins, in the towel cupboard – but there was no sign of her.

"Perhaps she slipped into the waiting area to get away from all the noise," Natalie suggested.

"Has anyone seen a gold-and-white long-haired chihuahua?" Tristan called as Andi led the way into the waiting area.

"No, sorry," a woman replied. Everyone else shook their head.

"Let's try the kennels," Andi said.

They pelted down the corridor, passing David and Aggie, who were clearly having a tense conversation. A cocker spaniel jumped up at the door of his pen and barked as they raced into the kennels.

Andi threw open the door of an empty pen near the window. She could see that Honey wasn't in there, but perhaps she was hiding under the quilt. She turned it over. Nothing.

Natalie and Tristan checked the other pens. Again, nothing.

"She's not in the salon . . . or the waiting room . . . or the kennels . . ." Andi said in a shaky voice. "Honey's gone!"

Chapter Nine

Two police officers, a young woman with short brown hair and a rather stocky man with blond hair and a neat beard, arrived at the grooming parlour. David had called them.

"My show-dog has been stolen," he explained. "She's a long-haired chihuahua." He was very pale and Andi's heart went out to him. She'd felt exactly the same when Buddy had disappeared during her first few days in Aldcliffe.

Tristan sat on a stool in the corner of the salon with his head in his hands. "This is all my fault."

Andi slipped an arm round his shoulders, not knowing what to say.

"We'll need to take statements from everybody,"

the policeman said. "And it would be best to close the salon for the rest of the day. Has anybody left since the incident?"

"A few people," Aggie admitted.

"I can give you the names of everyone who was here." Lena flipped open the appointment book.

Aggie came over to the Pet Finders.

"I'm sorry, Aggie." Tristan shook his head. "If only I hadn't been running after that woman . . ." He trailed off.

"Listen, Tristan," she said, patting his arm. "You tripped over a lead. It was an accident. It could have happened to any one of us."

"Can I have another word with you, please, Ms Patel?" the policeman called.

Aggie went back to speak to him.

The customers who'd been waiting for their pets to be groomed gave their names to the policewoman then left the salon, still talking about what had happened.

"Where do you think Honey's gone?" Natalie asked Andi. "Do you think she really *was* stolen?"

"Perhaps she ran outside. The door was open and she's small enough to have darted out without anyone noticing."

Tristan sat up straighter on his stool. "Suppose she *was* stolen. Who would want to steal her?"

"Honey's a champion show-dog," Andi pointed out. "She must be worth a lot of money."

"What's the good of stealing a show-dog if you can't put her in shows?" Natalie said. "Surely everyone would recognize her?"

"Another show-dog-owner might want to take her," Tristan said slowly. "Especially if Honey was a big rival to their dog."

Andi gasped. "Windwhistle! Amanda Slinger was in here earlier."

"I need to find out where she lives," Tristan said, sounding determined. "I started all this, so it's up to me to sort it out."

"*Us*, you mean," Natalie reminded him. "You're not in this by yourself."

"Did I hear you say that Honey's got a rival?" asked the policewoman, walking over.

"Windwhistle. He and Honey are favourites

104

to win in next Saturday's pet show," Natalie told her.

"Amanda Slinger is Windwhistle's owner," Andi added. "She called in to the salon just before the . . . er . . . incident."

The policewoman added Mrs Slinger's name to the list of customers. "We'll definitely need to interview her." She went to tell her partner.

"Mrs Slinger's our main suspect," Tristan said in a low voice. "But if the police are going to interview her, we should probably start somewhere else."

Natalie frowned. "Where?"

"Outside," Andi said. "There's a chance that Honey could have slipped out."

"I hope you're right," Tristan said. "A lost dog is easier to find than a stolen one."

The Pet Finders headed out of the salon and on to the pavement. "Where would a frightened chihuahua hide?" Andi wondered, looking up and down the road.

"Anywhere that she wouldn't get stepped on." Tristan crouched down to peer underneath a parked car. "She's not under here, but we should check all the cars."

They worked their way along the street, looking under every car: there was nowhere else to look because the buildings were set right on the pavement, with no front gardens where a tiny dog could lose herself among the plants.

Soon they came to a narrow alley. At the far end they could see traffic rushing by on the high street. "I hope she didn't go down there," Andi said.

"We should check," Tristan said. They trooped down the alley and burst out on to the high street, startling a few shoppers.

"There's no sign of Honey," Andi said. "Let's try in the shops." The Pet Finders split up to ask some shop-owners if they had seen Honey, but no one had.

The kids searched until the shops closed, then walked home slowly. "If she'd run out of the salon, surely we'd have found her by now," Natalie said.

"It looks as though someone *must* have taken her," Andi admitted. "I know Amanda Slinger is our main

suspect, but we don't know where she lives so we can't investigate her tonight. And there were a lot of other customers at Clip 'n' Curl who could have taken Honey."

"What about the lady with the parrot badges? Perhaps that's why she didn't stop when I called," Tristan suggested.

"But that was *before* the commotion in the salon," Andi said. "Honey was still with Lena then, having her nails clipped."

"Oh yeah," Tristan said. "So who else could have taken her? Someone with a bag, otherwise they'd have been seen carrying her outside."

"I don't know," Natalie said. "She's so small. You said Honey could fit in a pocket when we first met her."

"I was only joking. She's tiny, but not *that* tiny. There's no way she'd fit in a pocket." Tristan kicked an empty can that lay on the pavement and sent it clattering along the road. "So who *did* have a bag big enough to hold a chihuahua?"

"Amanda Slinger!" Andi remembered. "She was carrying Windwhistle's pet-carrier. I assumed

Windwhistle was inside, but I didn't actually see him. Perhaps she brought it in empty so she could steal Honey and stop her from being in the pet show."

"But how did she know Honey was there?" Natalie asked.

Andi shrugged. "She could have been keeping watch and seen David take her in. Or perhaps she had a peek at the appointment book. It wouldn't be hard – especially as Aggie, Joe and Lena have been so busy."

"We've got to search Amanda Slinger's house," Tristan said.

"But we don't know her address," Natalie reminded him.

"We can ask at Clip 'n' Curl tomorrow," Andi said.

"Or we can stop at Paws for Thought and ask Christine," Tristan suggested. "Amanda's a customer so she might know it."

Andi glanced at her watch and gasped. "Oh no! I promised Mum I'd be in early tonight. I've got to go. See you!" She sped away.

"I'm going to keep looking," Tristan called after her. "I'll ring you if I find Honey."

The next day after school, the Pet Finders headed straight for Paws for Thought to see how Christine was getting on with the pet show preparations, and to see if she had heard any news about Honey.

"Let's go to Clip 'n' Curl, too," Natalie suggested. "Aggie might know how the police investigation's going."

"I can't show my face at Clip 'n' Curl," Tristan said hurriedly. "Not after yesterday."

"What happened yesterday?" Ella asked from behind them.

Natalie put her hands on her hips. "Are you following us, Ella?"

Tristan blushed and quickly knelt down to re-tie his trainer lace. Andi could tell he was totally embarrassed.

"One of the dogs – a chihuahua – disappeared after a commotion," Andi said, shooting a warning glance at Natalie to stop her from blurting out Tristan's part in it.

"Oh." Ella's eyes stretched wide. "We should look for her."

"We *have*," Natalie said. "We're the Pet Finders. That's what we do. Come on, Tris." She tapped him with her foot. "Isn't that lace tied yet? We need to get a move on."

"Can I come along?" Ella asked.

"Of course you can!" Tristan piped up, much to Natalie's obvious dismay.

"Good! Are we going to be investigating the missing chihuahua? I'm really good at finding stuff. I once found my mum's wedding ring that had been lost for days. It was . . ."

"That's all we need," Natalie mumbled to Andi. "More of Ella's non-stop stories!"

When they reached Paws for Thought, Ella stopped outside. "Look at this!" she exclaimed. "The owner of this shop *must* be the thief!"

"Of course she's not!" Natalie snapped. "Christine's our friend."

"But she's got a card in her window advertising a long-haired chihuahua for sale. She's probably got the dog locked up in a back room or somewhere," Ella speculated.

"I'm not sure the thief would be that open about

selling Honey," Andi said gently. "I mean, if you'd stolen a valuable show-dog, you'd hardly put up a postcard to advertise the fact."

"Even if it wasn't Christine who wrote out the card," Ella said, "we should still ask who put it up. It could be a clue."

"She does have a point," Tristan admitted.

Andi had to agree. "OK. Let's check."

Inside the shop, Christine was on the phone and Max was lying in his usual spot in the window display, between a cat bed and an arrangement of leads. He jumped down to see them, his tail wagging. Andi found a dog treat in her pocket for him. Then he ambled back to the window, squeezing past a display of dog-food tins before flopping down again.

Ella was over by the counter talking to Christine, who had finished her phone conversation. "The card was put there by Scott Carling, a reputable chihuahua-breeder," Christine was saying. "There's no way he'd be mixed up in Honey's disappearance. He's a good friend of mine."

Natalie nudged Andi. "Why doesn't Ella keep

out of this? She's got no right to accuse Christine of anything."

Tristan sprang to Ella's defence. "She's just wants to help."

Natalie didn't say any more, but Andi could tell that she was almost at the end of her patience. She bit her lip, hoping Natalie wouldn't lose her temper. She wasn't exactly famous for being diplomatic!

"Is there any news of Honey, Christine?" she asked, going over to the counter.

"No. I spoke to Aggie earlier. David Nazrallah's very upset, understandably. To be honest, the whole thing is turning into a disaster – not just for David and Honey, but for the pet show, too. I've had several calls today from people who want to cancel their entries. They won't risk bringing their pets here if there's a dog-thief in the area." She sighed and ran a hand through her dark-brown hair. "We were relying on some top names from the dog-showing world to pull in the crowds and put the Aldcliffe show on the map. Unfortunately some of the show categories will have to be cancelled if things go on like this."

"How did everyone find out so quickly?" Andi asked.

"Amanda Slinger's been telling them, apparently," Christine replied. "And it was in the local paper today, too." She showed them the article, with a photo of David standing sadly beside Honey's empty dog basket.

"I bet Mrs Slinger's trying to guarantee a win for Windwhistle by knocking out the competition," Natalie said.

"She won't have a class for her precious pooch to compete in if everyone pulls out," Tristan pointed out. "But we should definitely go and see her. Do you know her address, Christine?"

"Yes, but I don't want you making a nuisance of yourselves."

"Us? A nuisance?" Tristan protested innocently.

Christine laughed, the worry lines disappearing from her face for a moment. "It has been known. But I suppose you know what you're doing when it comes to missing pets. And besides, you can save me a trip. I've got a herbal diet supplement to deliver to her."

"Perfect!" Natalie exclaimed. "Let's get over there straight away."

Chapter Ten

"Let's pick up Buddy and Jet on the way to Mrs Slinger's house," Andi suggested. "They'll enjoy the exercise, and having them with us will show Mrs Slinger that we're dog-lovers too. Perhaps she'll let us come in and play with Windwhistle."

"I wish I could come with you, but I've got to finish my history project," Ella said. "See you later!" She turned and headed in the opposite direction.

"She must love history," Tristan remarked. "Our project's not due in until next week."

Buddy and Jet loved meeting up for the walk to Amanda Slinger's house. They bounded around each other so energetically that their leads became tangled and the Pet Finders had to keep stopping to sort them out.

Amanda Slinger lived in a modern, flat-roofed house set behind a high wall. "Wow!" Natalie gasped as they went in through the wrought-iron gate. The front wall of the house was made entirely of mirrored glass, which reflected a spectacular fountain in the middle of the front garden.

As they drew nearer, Natalie checked her reflection in one of the windows. She smoothed her jacket and tucked a strand of blonde hair behind one ear.

The main entrance was at the side of the building, along a narrow path made of violet-grey slate chippings. Amanda Slinger answered their knock.

"We've brought Windwhistle's herbal diet supplement from Paws for Thought," Andi said. She handed the packet over, and then moved to one side so she could see past Mrs Slinger and into the house.

"Thank you." Mrs Slinger moved slightly,

blocking Andi's view. She looked as though she was about to close the door.

"Nice house," Tristan jumped in. "Have you ever thought of selling it? My parents are estate agents."

"We like it here, thank you. My husband and I had it built to our own design three years ago. Now, if there's nothing else . . ."

"Can we see Windwhistle?" Natalie said hurriedly. "We really love dogs."

"I'm afraid not," Mrs Slinger said.

That's suspicious, Andi thought. *Why would she stop us from coming in if she's got nothing to hide?*

"Some dogs try to pick fights with Windwhistle and he is far too small to defend himself," Mrs Slinger went on.

"I don't mind waiting out here with the dogs," Natalie volunteered.

"Oh. Well, in that case . . ." Mrs Slinger opened the door wide.

Andi handed Buddy's lead to Natalie and followed Tristan inside.

The main room of the house was huge, with a gleaming, professional-looking kitchen with brushed-steel worktops and three cream leather sofas arranged around a low table made from what looked like a slab of tree trunk. To Andi's disappointment, there was no sign of Honey.

Mrs Slinger ushered them into a smaller but equally luxurious room. "This is Windwhistle's space," she said.

Tristan raised his eyebrows and shot Andi a look that said very plainly that giving a dog a room of its own was taking things way too far. Luckily, Mrs Slinger didn't notice.

Windwhistle was lying on a low couch covered in a thick sheepskin rug. On the wall behind him were shelves and shelves of dog toys, feeding bowls, and collars and leads in every colour of the rainbow. His white pet-carrier stood in the corner – but Andi could see right inside it and Honey wasn't there.

The dog sat up and looked them over. Then he jumped down and trotted to greet them, lifting his feet daintily and wagging his fluffy tail.

"He's very cute," Andi said, kneeling on the deep, pale-blue carpet to stroke him. Windwhistle rolled over so she could rub his tummy. His fur felt as soft as down. "Aren't you lucky, having all these fabulous toys?" she told him.

"Nothing but the best for my little poppet," Mrs Slinger said proudly.

Tristan sidled over to the couch and casually lifted the rug to check that Honey wasn't hidden in its folds.

"What are you doing?" Mrs Slinger asked, her eyes narrowing.

"I . . . um . . . I was just feeling how soft this rug is. Windwhistle must love it."

"Yes." Mrs Slinger relaxed. "It's his favourite place to sleep."

"My dog likes lying on my bed," Andi said, wondering if they could find an excuse for going upstairs.

"Windwhistle spends quite a lot of time upstairs," Mrs Slinger said. "Especially if I have to go out without him. But this room is his pride and joy. He always comes in here when I'm cooking so that he can be near me. I don't allow him in the kitchen area — not since that horrible accident with the tomato sauce."

Tristan came to kneel beside Andi. He rubbed Windwhistle's chest gently. "It's terrible about poor Honey disappearing like that, isn't it?" he said, trying to move the conversation along.

"Oh, it is," agreed Mrs Slinger. "I'm so worried that Windwhistle might vanish next. Perhaps the thief is targeting chihuahuas. I've had extra locks fitted on all my windows and I've got the police station's number next to my phone so I can contact them immediately if anything happens."

"That should keep him safe," Tristan said. He leant close to Andi and whispered, "I've got a feeling she didn't take Honey. It's another dead end."

"If we could only check upstairs, too," Andi replied, equally quietly, "just so we can be sure Honey's not here." She raised her voice. "You've got a beautiful house, Mrs Slinger."

"Would you like to see the rest of it?" Amanda Slinger said, to Andi's relief. "It was featured in an issue of *Stunning Homes*, and the master suite won their Best Bedroom Award."

"That would be great," Andi said honestly.

Mrs Slinger led them across the main room and up a glass staircase. There were three bedrooms all decorated in varying shades of blue, with deep carpets and mounds of silk cushions on the beds.

"Honey's definitely not here," Andi whispered when they had seen all the rooms. Apart from two portraits of Windwhistle – one at the top of the stairs and one in the master bedroom – there was nothing doggy upstairs at all. Every window had a lock fitted, too. A large sheet of paper with a phone number and the words POLICE STATION written on it was taped to the wall by the phone in the master bedroom. It looked as though Amanda Slinger had been telling the truth when she'd said she was afraid that Windwhistle might be stolen, too.

"Thank you for showing us your house and for letting us see Windwhistle, Mrs Slinger," Andi said as they walked to the front door.

"You're welcome. Come again if you like," she said and let them out.

Natalie listened eagerly while they told her everything they'd found out.

"I'm sure she's not involved," Tristan said. "She must have put in those window locks to protect Windwhistle, like she said — I had a look at them and they're very shiny and new."

"We're getting nowhere," Natalie sighed. "We don't even know for sure whether Honey is lost or stolen. If she ran out of the salon on her own, why didn't we find her when we searched the area? She'd only been missing for about twenty minutes so she couldn't have gone far."

"And if she *has* been stolen," Tristan said, "then who took her? We've eliminated our only suspect."

"We'll have to come up with a new lead," Andi said. "And we'd better do it quickly, or Honey won't be back in time for the pet show."

When Andi arrived home, her mum came out to the hall to meet her. "Good news, Andi! Your parrot's owner phoned. She saw your posters. She says the bird's name is Bertie."

"That's brilliant!" Andi whooped. "Did she say how Bertie got out?"

123

"She's just moved to Aldcliffe, apparently. One of the removal men knocked over the parrot cage while he was moving furniture. The cage door opened and Bertie flew away. His owner's name is Claire Snowdon and she's coming to your school in the morning to pick him up."

Andi was thrilled. At least they'd managed to solve one of their cases, and now they'd have more time for finding Honey. And with the way things were going, the Pet Finders Club was going to need all the spare hours they could get!

Andi, Natalie and Tristan arrived at school a little earlier than usual the next morning. They wanted to say a last goodbye to Charlie before Claire Snowdon came to collect him.

"You're going home, Charlie," Andi said, reaching through the bars of the cage to stroke the parrot's soft chest-feathers.

The classroom door opened and Ms McNicholas came in. She was followed by a woman in her mid-thirties with long brown hair and a hand-knitted jumper worn over paint-stained jeans.

"I'll be sorry to see Charlie go," Natalie said, watching Ms Snowdon's face break into a smile when she saw the parrot.

"Me too. But not as sorry as Ms McNicholas," Tristan added. The teacher's eyes were red and puffy.

"It'll be good for Charlie to go home, though," Andi reminded them.

"These are the children who made the posters about Charlie . . . I mean, Bertie." Ms McNicholas motioned for them to come over to meet Ms Snowdon.

"Thank you," said Ms Snowdon. "I don't know how I would have found Bertie if it hadn't been for you."

"That's OK," Andi said. She looked at Ms Snowdon's jeans. "You look as though you've been decorating."

"Yes. We've . . . um . . . just moved here."

"You don't seem to have any spots of red paint, though," Natalie said lightly. "Didn't you want to take Bertie's advice?"

"Advice?" Ms Snowdon stared at Natalie as

though she was from another planet. "What do you mean, advice?"

"To paint it red," Natalie said.

Ms Snowdon looked baffled.

"It's one of the things Bertie says," Tristan added.

Andi began to feel uneasy. Surely Ms Snowdon must have heard the parrot speaking.

At that moment, Bertie spread his wings inside his cage. "Aak! Adam and Eve on a raft!" he squawked.

Ms Snowdon nearly jumped out of her skin.

The Pet Finders exchanged suspicious glances. "Do you think she's really his owner?" Andi whispered, drawing Natalie and Tristan aside.

"Just what I was thinking," Natalie replied in a low voice. "Parrots are pretty valuable. Perhaps she made up her mind to steal him after she saw the posters."

"Adam and Eve on a raft!" the parrot cried again.

"I suppose you must do a lot of rafting," Andi said to Ms Snowdon.

"Rafting?" Ms Snowdon gave a nervous laugh. "Oh, yes. I'm always out on the water. I take the bird with me. That's why he talks about being on a raft."

Andi's doubts about Claire Snowdon grew. Adam and Eve on a raft meant two eggs on toast; it had nothing to do with rafting.

"Would you mind just describing the charm on the parrot's leg?" Andi asked. "You know, as a security check before you take him home." She was suddenly glad that Natalie's mobile phone photo of the parrot had been a bit blurry. Only someone who really knew the parrot would be able to describe the palm tree.

Tristan stepped in front of the cage so Ms Snowdon couldn't see the bird.

The colour drained from Ms Snowdon's face. "A charm. Yes, of course. It's . . . um . . . gold. Well, a sort of silvery-goldy colour."

"And what shape is it?" Natalie prompted.

Ms McNicholas was staring at the Pet Finders in open-mouthed surprise, but she didn't say anything to stop them.

"Well, I . . ." Looking flustered, Ms Snowdon peered over Tristan's shoulder towards the parrot

cage, but Andi knew she was too far away to see the charm clearly. "I'm sorry, I appear to have made a mistake," the woman said suddenly. "It's not my parrot, after all." She turned and ran out of the door, barging past Ms McNicholas in her haste to get away.

"Thank goodness you realized she wasn't the owner." Ms McNicholas hurried to the cage to stroke the parrot. "If you hadn't been in the classroom, I'd have handed Charlie over to Ms Snowdon without checking if she really was his owner. Who knows what would have happened to him!"

"We had a case a bit like this a little while ago," Andi told her, "when someone rang up asking for payment in return for a lost Dalmatian. He didn't have the dog at all – he just wanted the owners to send him a cheque."

The bell rang for the start of school. "I'd better run down to the office and ring Fisher," Ms McNicholas said. "He needs to know that a would-be parrot-thief is in the area." She hurried out of the classroom.

129

"I'd better go, too," Tristan said.

Andi and Natalie headed for their seats. "It was lucky we worked out what Ms Snowdon was up to," Natalie said, "but poor Charlie still hasn't got a real owner."

"Yeah, but at least he's got a nice cage to live in," Andi said. "Poor little Honey could be anywhere!"

After school, the Pet Finders rushed back to Andi's house to make posters for Honey. Andi typed HELP HONEY! at the top of the page in large letters. Underneath it she added, *Lost: long-haired chihuahua.* They found a photo of the tiny dog on David Nazrallah's website and pasted it into the poster, then added Andi's phone number.

"If she *is* lost, these should do the trick," Andi said as the posters spooled out of the printer. "Honey is so eye-catching, she must have been spotted by someone." She sighed. "The posters won't be much help if someone stole her, though."

As soon as the posters were printed, the Pet Finders sped down to the high street and began taping them to lampposts and parking signs. They searched for Honey as they went along, calling her name, peering under parked cars and behind tubs of flowers, and scouting down narrow service alleys that ran beside shops. Andi felt her stomach tightening anxiously with every step they took. Honey was so tiny. How could she survive out here with no one to look after her?

The sky darkened and a pale moon appeared. "We're going to have to give up for tonight," Tristan said glumly. "We'll never find her in the dark."

Natalie sighed. "Poor Honey will have to spend another night outdoors – unless a dognapper's got her."

Andi shivered. She couldn't decide which was worse.

As they headed back the way they'd come they heard footsteps pounding towards them from behind. Turning, they saw Hannah Ling. Hannah's mum, Amy, ran the delicatessen next to Paws for Thought.

"Wait!" Hannah said, panting. She grabbed Andi's sleeve.

"What's up?" Andi asked.

"That missing dog," Hannah gasped. "The one on your posters. It's in the yard behind our shop!"

Chapter Eleven

The Pet Finders charged along the high street after Hannah, veered into the deli's side alley and arrived in the yard gasping for breath. Hannah's mum was standing in the back doorway, shining a torch on a pile of empty cardboard boxes. "She's still in there," Mrs Ling said in a low voice. "One of the boxes just moved." She handed the torch to Tristan. "Be careful."

"It's OK," Tristan replied. "I know it's not safe to rush up to a strange dog, but Honey should recognize me."

The Pet Finders tiptoed towards the boxes. "Honey!" Andi called. "Here, girl."

The beam picked up a patch of tan fur. "I think I can see her," Natalie breathed.

The tiny dog shrank down behind a box.

"It's OK, Honey," Andi reassured her. "We've come to help you." She leant forward and shifted the box a little. "Shine the light closer, Tris."

Tristan held the torch higher. Andi and Natalie took a peek behind the box and gasped.

"What's wrong?" Hannah cried.

"It's not Honey. It's a tan puppy," Natalie said, her voice heavy with disappointment.

Then a deep growl sounded behind them.

Andi whirled round and saw a large, fierce-looking dog standing in the gateway to the alley. She gulped.

"It's the same colour as the pup," Tristan whispered. "It must be the mother."

"We've got to get out of her way," Andi whispered back. "She probably thinks we'll hurt her baby." The Pet Finders backed away from the dog and her puppy, edging slowly towards the deli's back door so that the dog wouldn't think they were a threat.

The mother gave another growl, then padded past them to pick up the puppy. She gently gripped the scruff of its neck in her teeth and trotted out of the garden.

"She's so thin," Tristan said. "She must be a stray. Come on, we've got to follow her so Fisher can fetch her. She needs someone to look after her and her puppy."

The Pet Finders and Hannah tracked the dogs from a safe distance.

"I'll ring Fisher," Natalie said, pulling out her mobile.

The dog trotted along the high street with the puppy dangling from her mouth. Then she turned into a quiet side street. As Andi and her friends reached the corner they saw the dog slip between a rubbish skip and a high wall.

"What's she doing?" Tristan wondered, shining the torch towards the gap. The beam of light showed a shadowy space littered with rubbish. A rusty shopping trolley lay on its side amid tattered sheets of newspaper, dented drink cans and empty bottles. The dog settled her puppy inside the shopping trolley.

"She's got three other pups in there already,"

Andi gasped, standing on tiptoe to get a better view. "Oh, they're so cute!"

"Fisher's on his way," Natalie said, flipping her phone shut and coming to stand by Andi so she could see the pups.

"This is so exciting!" Hannah said, staring so hard at the family of dogs that she could have been under an eye-binding spell. "Pet-finding is fantastic!"

"It is," Andi agreed. "Or it is when it works out, anyway." Though she was glad to think that they were helping this poor stray dog and her puppies, she couldn't forget the fact that Honey was still missing.

The Pet Finders kept watch while they waited for Fisher to arrive. They didn't want the dog to run off with her puppies when help was on its way, although they knew they couldn't stop her if she decided to move. It could be dangerous to approach a strange dog, especially when it might have had bad experiences with people.

After about ten minutes, the RSPCA van turned into the alley, its headlights illuminating the buildings and the skip. Andi blinked and raised her hand to shield her eyes.

Fisher parked next to the skip. "Where are they?" he asked as he climbed out. He was holding a dog-catching pole with a noose at one end.

"Behind there," Tristan said, pointing to the skip.

"You four stay back," Fisher warned. He took a bowl of dog food from the passenger seat of the van and placed it close to the skip. "Here, girl," he called softly. Then he stood back and waited to see what would happen.

Andi held her breath as the dog emerged from behind the skip and cautiously approached the bowl. As soon as she reached the food she started to wolf it down.

"Poor thing," Fisher commented. "She's starving." He took a step towards the dog, holding out the pole. "Good girl. You eat up."

The dog jumped back and Fisher froze.

After eyeing him nervously for a few seconds, she slunk back to the bowl for another mouthful.

"That's it, girl," Fisher said, inching towards her again.

The dog stopped eating and watched him again, but this time she didn't move away.

Fisher crept forward until he was close enough to use the dog-catching device. Slowly lowering the pole, he slipped the noose over the dog's head. When she realized what had happened she tried to run off, but the noose tightened around her neck until it was as snug as an ordinary collar. "Good girl," Fisher said calmly. "Don't worry, you're safe now." He led her towards the van.

The dog struggled to break free, but Fisher held the pole tightly and guided her into the travelling cage.

"You stay there while I fetch your pups," he said, loosening the noose, then slipping it off. He quickly shut the cage door to prevent her from escaping.

The dog howled pitifully as Fisher squeezed behind the skip. He emerged a few seconds later with two puppies cradled against his chest. They were thin and dirty, and even from this distance Andi could see that they were shivering. "I think we found them just in time," she said to Hannah. "Thank goodness you spotted that puppy."

"I went to look for Honey out in my yard because I saw your poster," Hannah explained as Fisher carried the puppies to the van. "I really thought I'd found her!"

The dog stopped howling when she saw her pups. She watched anxiously as Fisher placed them in the next travelling cage, then lay down with her nose against the bars that separated her from her babies.

Fisher returned to the shopping trolley and brought out the last two pups and put them with the rest. "You did a great job," he said. "We'll keep them at the centre until they're stronger, then we'll find them homes. They're so cute I don't think we'll have any problem placing them." He climbed into the driver's seat of the van. "See you."

The Pet Finders and Hannah returned to the deli to make sure there were no more puppies anywhere around. "Look," Andi said as they poked through the boxes. "Here's an old blanket. This must be where the dog had her babies."

"I wonder why she decided to move them," Tristan mused.

"We're having a new storeroom built," Hannah said. "My dad's been shifting stuff out of the yard all day to make room for it. I expect the mother dog thought it wasn't a safe place for her babies any more."

"It's been a really exciting evening," Natalie said. "The only thing is, it hasn't brought us any closer to finding poor Honey."

On Friday, the Pet Finders and Ella met up in the school playground during morning break. It was dotted with puddles that reflected the dull grey sky. "The pet show is tomorrow," Tristan said, turning up his collar against the cold wind, "and we haven't found Honey yet." They'd searched every street within two miles of Clip 'n' Curl and displayed at least fifty posters, but the chihuahua seemed to have vanished into thin air.

"I went into Clip 'n' Curl yesterday," Natalie said. "I thought it was worth checking the appointment book for the day Honey disappeared."

"Did you find out anything useful?" Andi asked. She'd intended to go to the grooming salon herself, but keeping up with all the homework Ms McNicholas was dishing out and trying to teach Buddy his trick had meant she'd had hardly a moment of free time.

Natalie shook her head. "There were loads of appointments that day, but we already knew that. And none of the customers seem suspicious. Aggie knows most of them and she's sure they wouldn't have stolen Honey. The only ones she hadn't seen before were an old lady who's nearly blind – she's got a pug so fat it can hardly walk, Aggie said – and an eight-year-old girl with an enormous crossbreed."

Tristan sighed. "Neither of them sounds like dognappers."

"What if Aggie stole Honey herself?" Ella said. "Or perhaps it was someone else who works in the salon. Perhaps one of them has always wanted a dog of their own and can't afford to buy one."

"Aggie, Lena and Joe wouldn't steal a dog," Natalie retorted. "You should get your facts straight before you start accusing people, Ella. Christine was really upset when you—"

"Ella's only trying to help," Andi said, shooting Natalie a warning look. It was going to take a team effort – including Ella's help – to solve both cases.

"We haven't found Charlie's owners, either," Tristan pointed out as if he had read Andi's mind. They'd stopped working through the café lists when Ms Snowdon phoned Andi's mum. The delay meant they still had loads of cafés to ring.

"Perhaps we could concentrate on calling places with a tropical name," Andi suggested. "To tie in with Charlie's palm tree charm."

"That's a good idea!" Ella exclaimed. "Anywhere with 'Caribbean' or 'island' in the name would be a good place to start. Did I ever tell you about the holiday I had in the Caribbean?"

Just then, a rainbow-coloured van pulled up outside the school.

"What's Jango doing here?" Tristan wondered.

They watched as Jango Pearce climbed out of his van, opened the back door and took out several large boxes.

"Looks like he's brought you a little snack, Tris," Natalie teased.

"I wish," Tristan said. "Let's go and see what he's up to."

"Hello, Jango," Andi called.

"Hi, there," he called back. His grey hair stood on end, and he looked a little flustered. "I'm running late today because the chap on the till at the cash-and-carry kept asking if I'd found my parrot."

"You've lost Long John Silver?" Andi asked, shocked.

"No. He's marching up and down my counter just the same as ever. I kept telling the chap it wasn't my parrot had gone missing, but he wouldn't listen."

The Pet Finders looked at each other. "Perhaps he heard about another customer losing their parrot and thought it was you," Natalie guessed. "Everyone in Aldcliffe knows you've got a parrot."

"There must be other cafés with parrots," Jango grumbled. "Why doesn't the cash-and-carry chap pester *their* owners?"

"That's right!" Tristan exclaimed. "If Charlie's owner runs a café then he or she has to buy stock from a cash-and-carry. Perhaps it's the same one that Jango uses." He clutched Andi's arm. "We've got to go there."

"Where is the cash-and-carry, Jango?" said Andi.

"On the main road about half a mile out of town. Now, let me get these brownies to your dinner supervisor. She must be wondering what's happened to them. See you."

"Bye, Jango," the kids chorused.

"We've got to tell Ms McNicholas about this new lead," Andi said. "Come on!"

At lunchtime, the Pet Finders piled into Ms McNicholas's sports car for the trip to the cash-and-carry. The teacher had asked the head for permission to take them out of school for an hour. There was no room for Ella in the car but she didn't seem to mind. "Tell me all about it when you get back," she called as Ms McNicholas started the engine. "And I'll finish telling you about my Caribbean holiday!"

"How come you're in the front again, Tristan?" Natalie complained as they sped through town. "It should be your turn to be squashed in the back with Andi."

"Or with *you*," Andi told Natalie. "I haven't had a turn in the front yet either."

"I'm saving you two from having an argument about who gets to sit here," Tristan said, settling more comfortably into the seat.

Natalie swiped the back of his head and Andi laughed. The gloom she'd felt earlier had vanished as soon as Jango had given them this new lead.

Ms McNicholas pulled up in front of the cash-and-carry, and they all piled out of the car and into the building. The place was quiet and the checkout man was reading a newspaper.

"Can we ask you about a lost parrot, please?" Andi began.

The man looked up. He was heavily built, with folds of skin around his chin and neck which reminded Andi of a bloodhound. "Not another one!" he said, laying down the newspaper. "Everyone's losing parrots lately."

"Actually, we've found one," Natalie said. "Jango Pearce said you'd been talking about someone who lost one."

"Yeah. Maureen, the other cashier, was telling

146

me about it," the man said. "I thought it was Jango's, but it wasn't."

"Is that her?" Andi asked, pointing to a red-haired woman at the next counter.

"That's right. Hey, Maureen," he called. "These kids are asking about that missing parrot."

"We've found one," Tristan told Maureen.

The woman came over, smoothing down her brown overall. "A customer lost one a couple of weeks ago – the pineapple lady. I call her that because she bought so many pineapples. A hundred cases. Cleared us right out."

"Do you know her real name and address?" Andi asked.

"No, sorry. She had her own van so we didn't have to deliver. And she's not a regular customer. I'd never seen her before."

"Oh, no," Natalie groaned. "I really thought we were getting somewhere."

"We still are," Tristan said. "She bought loads of pineapples. That's got to be a clue."

"Yes." Andi nodded. "And we're almost positive that Charlie comes from a café."

"But a café that serves loads of pineapples?" Natalie asked, confused.

"Why not? The Banana Beach Café serves loads of bananas. So, perhaps Charlie's café has lots of pineapple on the menu!"

"Plus, pineapples are exotic, so they tie in with the palm tree charm on Charlie's leg. Perhaps the café's even got an exotic name." Andi did a little skip, feeling that this time they really *were* on to something. She took out the list of cafés that she'd been phoning. They'd divided the list alphabetically and Andi had the final third, from R to Z. So far, she'd only got up to V. Hurriedly she scanned the list.

"Here!" she cried, stabbing the last name with her finger. "Zebedee's Pineapple Paradise. This must be our parrot's home!"

Chapter Twelve

One phone call later, to the number at the very bottom of Andi's list, and the Pet Finders had found Charlie's owner, Krista da Joseph. Or *Zebedee's* owner, as it turned out. The kids were disappointed that Ms McNicholas wouldn't let them miss school so they could return Charlie to his home straight away. But at least she had agreed to drive them to Zebedee's Pineapple Paradise after school.

The afternoon crawled by. Andi found herself constantly glancing at the clock, but the hands seemed to be stuck in one place. At the end of the day, she and Natalie packed their rucksacks then raced to the teacher's desk. "Are you ready, Ms McNicholas?"

"Yes. Go and get Tristan, please," she said.

Andi and Natalie pelted to the door, intending to run to his classroom, but he was already waiting for them in the corridor, hopping from foot to foot.

Ms McNicholas picked up Charlie's cage and carried it out to the car, with the Pet Finders close behind. "I'll hold him on my lap while you drive, OK, Ms McNicholas?" Tristan said.

"Thank you, Tristan," Ms McNicholas replied, handing him the cage and taking out her car keys.

Tristan grinned at Andi and Natalie. "Looks like I'm in the front again. There's no room in the back for two people *and* a parrot cage."

"That was sneaky, Tris," Natalie fumed.

It didn't take long to cross Aldcliffe and they were soon pulling into Zebedee's car park on the edge of town.

"Look at the sign!" Natalie exclaimed. It was shaped like a palm tree – exactly like the charm on their parrot's leg.

Charlie began to squawk and flap his wings.

"I think he knows he's home," Andi said.

Ms McNicholas got out of the car, then came round to the passenger door and opened it. She looked as though she was fighting back tears as she took the cage from Tristan. Andi realized that the teacher was going to find it hard to say goodbye to the friendly bird.

"Oh no!" Tristan groaned. "I'm covered in parrot seed. And I'm wet. Charlie's water must have spilt." He climbed out of the car and began to brush his school trousers.

Natalie hooted with laughter. "What a shame!" She winked at Andi. "Perhaps you should have let one of us sit in front with the cage. That way you wouldn't look like a birdfeeder now."

They crossed the car park and went into the café, a large crowded room with a tropical island mural painted on the far wall. Every table held parrot-shaped salt-and-pepper shakers and there were two fake palm trees near the door. A large, empty parrot cage stood on the far end of the polished counter, which ran nearly the whole length of the café. Charlie squawked louder than ever and a woman came running out of the kitchen carrying a tray of pineapple slices.

"Zebedee!" she cried, her face lighting up. She dashed down the café and took the cage from Ms McNicholas. "I've been so worried, you naughty boy!"

She lifted the parrot out of the cage and let him walk up her arm and on to her shoulder, where he nuzzled her ear. "It's so good to have him home," she said, stroking his feathers. "If you stay here for a moment, I'll put Zebedee back in his cage, then I'll find you a table." She walked to the cage, but the parrot didn't want to go inside. Instead, he hopped up on to her head.

"Come on, boy," she said, reaching up to fetch him. "You can't fly around loose while the café's open. Some customers might not take too kindly to a parrot visiting their table. And I don't want you flying away again."

"Adam and Eve on a raft!" the parrot squawked as Krista shut him in his cage.

"I'm not surprised that you solve so many

missing-pet cases," Ms McNicholas said, smiling at the Pet Finders. "You should all be proud of yourselves."

Andi felt herself blush.

Krista came back with four pineapple-shaped menus. "You've just made me the happiest woman in the world. Order whatever you want. It's on the house!"

They sat at the table nearest the parrot's cage and watched him jumping from perch to perch as he got to know his old home again.

Andi opened her menu. "Look. All Charlie's – I mean, Zebedee's – phrases are here. A Short Lumberjack is three pancakes – and a tall one's a stack of six."

"And Hot Wax is here, too. It means cheese on toast," Tristan said.

"Here's a Hammer Slammer, too," added Ms McNicholas. "And Adam and Eve on a Raft."

Krista came back to take their orders.

"I'll have a hamburger with lettuce and onions, please," Andi said.

"Give me one hockey puck, take it through the

garden and pin a rose on it," Krista shouted to the chef.

"Paint it red! Aak!" Zebedee squawked.

Andi laughed. "How did he know I wanted ketchup on it?"

"Can I get you a pineapple juice, too?" Krista asked. "It's freshly squeezed. The best pineapple juice in Britain!"

"I'm really happy for Krista," Ms McNicholas said while they waited for the food to come, "but I'm going to miss having a parrot."

"Why don't you get a bird of your own?" Tristan suggested.

Ms McNicholas looked thoughtful. "Perhaps I will."

"It's good to have a pet," Andi said encouragingly. This case had turned out great, she thought, watching Zebedee tidy his feathers.

If they could just find Honey, things would be perfect . . .

The day of the pet show dawned grey and chilly, with a cold wind and the threat of rain. Andi woke up early. She'd arranged to take Buddy to Natalie's house to prepare for the show. They'd decided not to go to Clip 'n' Curl for their free doggie wash because Tristan was still feeling awkward about visiting the salon. Besides, it was hard to worry about how Buddy was going to do in the show when Honey was still missing.

The doorbell rang just after eight o'clock and Andi ran to answer it with Buddy at her heels. Tristan was on the step. Behind him, out on the pavement, stood Ella.

Andi's heart sank. She didn't dislike Ella, but she couldn't imagine Natalie being overjoyed to see her. "Hello, Andi," Tristan said. "Is Buddy ready for his big day?"

"Yeah. I'll just get his things." Andi had already put his shampoo, brush and comb in a carrier bag. Now she just had to pick up the hoop.

Mrs Talbot came into the hall to see them off. "Good luck!"

"Thanks." Andi kissed her mum, then grabbed her jacket, clipped on Buddy's lead and scooted out of the door.

Ella and Tristan walked behind Andi all the way to Natalie's house. At first Andi tried to get involved in the conversation but whenever she turned round to join in, Ella stopped, so there was always a distance between them. Andi was puzzled, but she decided Ella must want to talk to Tristan alone.

Natalie was waiting outside her house for them, with Jet on his lead. "We forgot to buy any ribbon for the dogs to wear round their necks," she said. "Let's scoot down to the high street now. We should have plenty of time."

This time, Ella stayed a few steps ahead of them as they walked, while the dogs bounced around them.

"I hate to think of the pet show going ahead without Honey," Natalie said. "And I hate to think of Windwhistle winning – it wouldn't be fair with Honey out of the running." She sighed. "I'm beginning to think this is one case we're not going to solve. We still can't be sure if Honey's lost or stolen."

"We know Amanda Slinger didn't take her," Tristan pointed out.

"And that the other customers aren't likely to be dognappers," Natalie added. "But if Honey ran out of the salon we would have found her. We've searched everywhere! She *must* have been stolen."

"I'm not so sure," Andi said. "Think about it. The commotion happened by accident, didn't it?"

"Too right," Tristan said. "So?"

"So it wasn't as though anybody had planned a distraction to steal Honey. And anyway, everyone was busy chasing their own dogs."

"That's true," Tristan said. "But if Honey hasn't been stolen, then why haven't we found her?"

"I've got an idea," Ella chimed in.

Andi held her breath, hoping Natalie wouldn't say anything.

"If the dog's as tiny as you say, she might have hidden somewhere in the shop!" Ella continued.

"We've already searched the salon," Natalie pointed out.

They turned into the high street, which was packed with people. Andi noticed a man coming towards her with an empty pet-carrier. She tried to move out of his way but the basket caught her painfully in the shins. "Ow!" She rubbed her legs.

"What a huge basket!" Tristan said. "He must have a massive dog."

Andi stared at him. She remembered the time Buddy had scared Amanda Slinger's tiny dog. Windwhistle had run into his pet-carrier for safety. Perhaps Honey did the same when she got scared. "Ella's right!" she exclaimed. "Honey might have hidden in one of the pet-carriers in the kennels. I didn't think to look inside them."

"But she'd have come out later, when things calmed down," Natalie pointed out.

"Perhaps she couldn't get out," Andi said. "Perhaps the door got wedged shut or something. We've got to check. Come on!"

Suddenly they heard a squeal. Whirling around, they saw a golden retriever jumping up at Ella. "Get it away from me," she begged, flailing her hands. "Please!"

The boy holding the dog's lead pulled it away. "Sorry. He's just being friendly," he said.

Ella put her hands over her face and burst into tears.

"What's wrong?" Andi gasped, running over. "Did the dog bite you?"

"Don't come near me. Not with Buddy." Ella lowered her hands and backed against a shop window, looking terrified.

"Buddy's not going to do anything to you." Natalie joined them, frowning. "Ella, are you scared of dogs?"

"I . . . I'm not scared exactly. I just haven't had any experience with animals. But I'm not afraid, just allergic. And I'm OK with fish."

"How does she know she's allergic if she's never had any experience with animals?" Natalie whispered to Andi.

Andi privately agreed, but she didn't say so. Ella was upset enough already.

"What about that stuff you said about helping out at the RSPCA?" Tristan put in.

Ella hung her head. "I made it up. I wanted to have something in common with you so you'd like me on my first day. Everything I know about animals, I found out on the Internet."

"We *do* like you," Andi said, ignoring Natalie's

glare. "You don't have to make things up."

"Come to Clip 'n' Curl with us anyway, Ella," Tristan urged. "You can wait outside if you don't want to be inside with all the pets. If Andi's right, Honey could have been in that carrier all week."

The Pet Finders charged over to the salon with Ella keeping a good distance from Buddy and Jet. When they arrived, David Nazrallah was standing just inside the door, his eyes blazing. In front of him, Aggie looked pale and worried.

"You'll hear from my solicitor about this!" David raged. He turned to leave.

"Wait, David. We think Honey might be here after all!" Andi cried.

She, Tristan and Natalie squeezed past him and raced along the corridor that led to the kennels. To their horror, the pet-carriers were gone.

Aggie, David and Ella came hurrying in. "What do you mean?" David asked. "How can Honey be here?"

"Where are all the pet-carriers?" Tristan demanded.

"There was a mix-up with the order," Aggie

replied. "The supplier sent too many. He came and picked up the extras on Wednesday morning."

"Oh no!" Andi gasped. "We think Honey could be inside one of them!"

Chapter Thirteen

The Pet Finders piled into the back of David's car and Ella jumped in the front. There wasn't a moment to lose!

Andi hugged Buddy tightly as they sped across town to the warehouse where the pet supplies were stored. It seemed to take ages to get through the busy Saturday traffic. *Please, please, please, let Honey be all right*, she wished silently.

At last they reached Fernham, a village that bordered Aldcliffe, and David wove through narrow lanes until they reached the warehouse.

"We'll probably have to split up to search," Ella said. "Warehouses can be enormous. I went to one with my dad once to get some stuff for the theatre he used to manage and we were there for hours trying to find everything we needed."

Andi wished Ella would be quiet. Telling them how hard it was to find anything in a warehouse wasn't exactly helpful.

David drove into the yard and jerked to a halt next to a sign that said BUTLER'S PET SUPPLIES. They all piled out. Andi's heart sank. The warehouse was huge – at least the size of an aircraft hangar, and the height of a two-storey building. How on earth were they going to find one tiny dog inside all the pet-carriers in there?

"Wait here, Bud." Andi lifted him back into the car. "Jet will keep you company. We won't be long." Buddy whined as she shut the door, but Andi knew she couldn't keep an eye on Buddy and search for Honey at the same time.

They sprinted across the yard and hammered on the warehouse door. A sign fastened to the wall showed that it was only open on weekdays between 10 am and 5 pm. "I hope there's someone here," Andi said anxiously.

"Open up!" Tristan yelled, banging harder than ever. "It's urgent!"

They heard bolts shooting back and the door opened, revealing an enormous warehouse full of metal shelving crammed with pet goods. The security guard, a skinny man in a blue shirt and navy trousers, peered at them. "What's up?"

"We think there may be a dog in here," Andi said breathlessly.

The guard frowned. "No, this is a pet supplies warehouse. We don't keep animals here."

"She got trapped in a pet-carrier by mistake," Natalie explained. "It was part of a batch that was picked up last week from a salon in Aldcliffe. Do you know where they are now?"

Good thinking, Nat, thought Andi. That should save searching the entire warehouse!

Still frowning, the security man shuffled back from the door and pointed into the shadows. "You could try Aisle 37," he said. "Left-hand side, about halfway down. We had some returns come in the other day and that was the only space left."

Andi, Tristan, Natalie and Ella sprinted past the

guard and raced along the aisles. 34, 35, 36 . . .

"This is it!" Tristan shouted, swerving sideways and vanishing between the high stacks of shelves.

Halfway down they found what they were looking for, right where the security man had said – shelf upon shelf of pet-carriers stretching all the way up to the ceiling. "Honey! Can you hear me?" Andi called, throwing open the nearest carrier.

Honey wasn't inside.

Pushing it aside, Andi pulled another carrier off the shelf. It was empty, too.

They all worked frantically, pulling down box after box, knowing that they were racing against the clock. If Honey had been trapped without food or water for four days, she would be in serious trouble. Andi flashed back to her search for the old hunting-dog, Tate. When they'd found him, he had crawled under a bush to die – but that was at the end of a very long and happy life. This wasn't the same at all. Honey had to be OK!

Every carrier she opened was empty. Andi grew more desperate by the second. "Honey, where are you, girl?" She paused for a moment to listen, but there was no answering whimper.

The bottom two shelves were soon empty and the third shelf was out of reach. "We'll need a ladder," David said.

"I'll get one." The security man raced away. To Andi's relief, he seemed to have understood the urgency of their search at last.

"There's no time." Andi scrambled on to a shelf at waist height then stretched up to grab a shelf support above her head.

"Careful, Andi," Natalie warned. "The shelves are wet in places. I think the roof must leak."

Andi hauled herself on to the third shelf. There wasn't much space in front of the pet-carriers and she held on tightly with one hand while passing baskets down with the other. Bit by bit, she cleared enough space to work in. Then she checked some carriers herself, shifting them to one side when she'd looked inside. When she reached the back of the shelf, she noticed a glitter of pink below her. "What's that?" she said, peering down.

The bottom shelf was about half a metre off the

floor and a bright-pink carrier had fallen down behind it. It was lying on its side, half in and half out of a puddle from the leaky roof. Andi slid down behind the shelves and picked it up. Her heart started thudding. This carrier definitely felt heavier than the others. Holding her breath, Andi opened the door.

Inside, lying very still with her eyes closed, was Honey.

"I've found her!" Andi called. With trembling fingers, she reached in, hoping for Honey's sake that she wasn't too late. The tiny dog felt warm and when Andi rubbed her fur, one eye flicked open and looked up at Andi.

"She's alive!" Andi cried. Cradling the tiny creature carefully against her chest, she crawled out through the lowest shelf. Honey was so thin, she felt like a baby bird in Andi's hand.

The security man came back with a stepladder. He stopped when he saw Honey. "Is she . . .?"

"Alive," David breathed.

At the sound of his voice, Honey opened her mouth and gave a little whimper.

David came over to take her gently in his hands. "Her fur's wet."

"Probably from the roof," the guard said. "The manager's been saying he'll get someone in to look at it for ages."

"Actually, he's saved Honey's life," Andi said. "The rainwater that soaked through her pet-carrier kept her alive. Animals can survive that long without food, but not water."

Natalie phoned ahead to tell Fisher that they were on their way. Then they all piled into the car and headed for the RSPCA centre.

"I saw a film once about a man who got trapped in a cave for two weeks. He survived by drinking rainwater just like Honey," Ella said chattily.

Fisher was waiting outside the RSPCA centre when David pulled up. "Come on in," he called. "We need to fix up a drip to re-hydrate Honey and give her some nutrients to make up for all the meals she's missed. There's no way she'll be fit enough for the pet show, I'm afraid."

David shook his head. "That's the last thing on my mind right now."

Andi glanced at her watch. "We'd better go. We haven't even started getting Buddy and Jet ready for the show yet."

Andi, Natalie, Tristan and Ella sped back to Natalie's house and found Aggie waiting for them. "Mobile dog-groomer at your service!"

"We found Honey and she's going to be OK," Natalie told her.

"I know. David phoned and asked me to help you out. So let's get these two into the bath." They ran upstairs with Ella trailing behind.

"Are you all right, Ella?" Tristan asked.

"Yeah. Buddy and Jet seem like nice dogs, but I'll watch what's going on from a distance, if that's OK."

The dogs were ready in record time. Jet's gleaming black fur showed off the red ribbon Aggie had tied round his neck. Buddy wore an emerald-green ribbon that looked perfect against his sleek tan-and-white fur.

"Wow, Bud," Andi said, hugging him. "You look amazing!"

"Good luck with the show," Ella called, as they hurried downstairs.

"Aren't you coming?" Tristan asked.

Ella shook her head. "I might start to feel more confident about dogs with Buddy and Jet to help me, but there'll be too many at the show. I'm not ready for that just yet."

"Thanks for helping us find Honey," Andi said as Ella opened the front door.

"That's all right. See you on Monday. Bye, Tristan." She gave him a huge smile, and then shut the door behind her.

"Phew," said Natalie. "All that non-stop talking drives me mad."

"She's only trying to be friendly," Andi pointed out.

"I know. And I suppose I can put up with her some of the time, but I don't want to hang around with her every second of the day. In any case, I'm not sure I want to spend too much time with someone who's got such bad taste."

"You said you liked her clothes," Andi reminded her.

Natalie grinned and nodded towards Tristan. "I was thinking more of her taste in boys!"

The pet show was in full swing when they arrived at the RSPCA centre for the second time that day. The hall, the car park and part of the football pitch next door had all been pressed into use for rings and collecting areas. "It doesn't seem to matter that some people pulled out," Tristan said. "There are still about a zillion here."

"And the sun's come out, too," Natalie said. "That's lucky because one of the show-rings is in the car park."

They squeezed through the crowd, admiring the beautifully-groomed dogs in their roomy show-cages. They recognized some of them from Clip 'n' Curl and from their Musical Freestyling class. The main show-ring had been set up at the end of the hall furthest from the door, with plenty of room around it for spectators.

"Junior Handler Class," announced a voice over the loudspeaker.

Andi gulped. Suddenly her stomach was full of butterflies, and her hands felt clammy on Buddy's lead. Was she about to make a total fool of herself and Bud? She took a deep breath and squared her shoulders. Buddy looked fabulous, and she'd practised his trick until he was probably dreaming about jumping through hoops. She couldn't let him down now. She crouched and patted Buddy's head. "That's us, boy."

Leaving Buddy's hoop with Tristan, she went into the ring. The other competitors looked super-confident, which made Andi even more nervous. So much for the RSPCA wanting to encourage brand new competitors to take part in dog shows – everyone else looked as though they'd been competing all their lives! A tall, slender girl with flowing blonde hair led an elegant Afghan that seemed a perfect match for her hairstyle, while behind her walked a very serious-looking boy with a bouncing black-and-white Border collie.

Andi decided she wasn't helping herself by studying the competition too closely. Following the boy in front, who had a beautiful Dalmatian, she walked round the ring with Buddy trotting obediently at her heels. Glancing sideways, she saw her mum, Tristan and Natalie standing at the edge of the ring. Her mum smiled encouragingly, while Natalie and Tris gave her a thumbs-up.

The judge watched intently from her place in the centre of the circle. "Line your dogs up, please," she called after two circuits.

Buddy sat on Andi's foot and she ruffled his ears, trying not to look at the crowd or at the judge as she worked her way along the row. She racked her brains to remember everything David Nazrallah had told her about showing dogs: give the judge plenty of time to look at your dog, and listen very carefully to instructions.

When the judge reached Buddy, she gave him a quick look over. "Very nice," she told Andi. Then she returned to the centre of the ring. "Please walk your dogs round the ring again," she told the contestants.

"Come on, Bud," Andi said.

"Left turn," called the judge.

Andi turned and was pleased when Buddy followed neatly.

"Fast pace," the judge said.

Andi sped up and Buddy ran with her. "Good boy," she whispered. They'd got off to a great start!

As they jogged around the end of the ring, she spotted David Nazrallah watching from the back of the crowd. He caught her eye and nodded, as if he thought she was doing well, too.

The judge studied the competitors while they ran, jogged, and walked around the ring, stopping or changing direction on her orders. Andi hardly noticed the other people in the ring: her attention was totally focused on Buddy. At last, the judge told them all to halt. "For a bit of fun," she explained to the spectators, "we have asked the competitors to work out a simple trick with their dog." She pointed to the boy with the Dalmatian. "Will you start, please?"

The boy led his dog on to the small stage to one side of the ring. He unclipped his dog's lead then put his hands down on the floor, forming a bridge with his body. He whistled and the Dalmatian wriggled underneath him, ran around him and, finally, jumped right over him. The crowd clapped enthusiastically as the boy stood up.

Uh-oh, Andi thought. *That was good. I hope Buddy remembers how to jump through the hoop.*

"You next, please," the judge said, smiling at Andi.

Andi ran across to Tristan with Buddy scampering beside her. She took the hoop from him. "Good luck," he called as she ran to the stage.

The butterflies in Andi's stomach started doing complicated gymnastics as she removed Buddy's lead. There was no turning back now! She held the hoop about ten centimetres off the ground. "Through you go, Bud."

Buddy wagged his tail and sat.

"No! No sitting," Andy whispered. "Come on, boy." She gestured for him to go through the hoop. He stood up, ran towards it then dodged around it.

A ripple of laughter ran through the crowd.

Andi's cheeks grew hot. "Come on, Buddy," she begged. "Don't embarrass me in front of all these people. I know you can do this."

Buddy ran at the hoop again, then squeezed underneath it.

The laughter swelled.

This was turning into a disaster!

Suddenly Andi remembered how she'd taught

Buddy to go through the hoop the first time. "Like this, boy," she said, trying desperately to stay calm. Trying to forget the watching crowd, she crouched down then jumped awkwardly through the hoop. To her relief, Buddy followed.

The crowd cheered, and as Andi took a bow, she spotted Ms McNicholas clapping from the edge of the arena. Andi gave Buddy a treat, then clipped on his lead and jumped down from the stage.

They returned to their place at the side of the ring and watched the remaining dogs perform their tricks. They all behaved perfectly. *We're going to be last by a mile*, Andi thought. "Never mind, Bud," she said as she led him out of the ring. "We did our best." He'd done brilliantly with the basic showing routine – they'd just run out of luck when it came to doing his trick. *Can dogs get stage fright?* Andi wondered.

When the judge announced the results, Andi and Bud didn't get first, second, or even third place. But Andi realized she didn't mind. It had been a lot of fun just being in the show. She clapped and whooped with genuine delight as the winners accepted their ribbons.

When all the prizes had been handed out, Andi started to follow the other competitors out of the ring, but the judge asked everyone to wait. "I'd like to award a rather unusual prize for this event," she announced. "The ribbon for the best *human* trick goes to Andi Talbot!"

Andi burst out laughing. "I bet I'm the first *person* who's ever won a prize at a dog show." She and Buddy headed for the stage, while the crowd clapped and clapped. Out of the corner of her eye, she could see her mum, Tristan and Natalie doing a miniature Mexican wave.

"Well done," the judge said, shaking hands with Andi and handing her a green-and-yellow striped ribbon. "I've never seen a person jump through a hoop instead of their dog!"

Andi thanked her, waved the ribbon at the crowd, then ran over to Natalie and Tristan.

"They judged the Best Condition class while you were in the ring," Natalie said, "and Jet came third." She showed Andi the yellow ribbon fastened to his collar.

"That's brilliant, Nat!" Andi exclaimed. "I'm not

surprised Jet did so well. His coat's so shiny I can almost see my face in it."

Tristan swapped his can of fizzy drink into his right hand and glanced at his watch. "They'll be judging the Best In Show outside," he said. "Come on, we can't miss that!"

As they ran outside, the loudspeaker boomed out: "The results of the Best In Show competition are ready."

"Quick!" Natalie exclaimed.

The Pet Finders darted across the car park to the outdoor ring. Through the crowd, they could see the six competitors who had already won their purebred classes standing in a line. Amanda Slinger and Windwhistle were among them.

"And the winner is . . . Windwhistle!" declared the announcer.

Everyone cheered and clapped, although privately Andi thought the ribbon would have been awarded to Honey if she had been able to take part. There was something about the little dog's personality that made her really special – and had probably given her the determination to survive while she was trapped in the carrier.

"There's David," Andi said, spotting him in the crowd.

The Pet Finders wriggled their way through to him.

"Andi, you did really well!" he greeted her, his brown eyes sparkling. "It was a shame Buddy decided he didn't want to jump through the hoop, but apart from that you looked like real professionals!"

"Thanks," said Andi. "Your advice worked, although I'm not sure Bud's got a great show-ring career ahead of him."

"How's Honey?" Tristan asked.

"Fisher thinks she might be able to go home later today," he said, sounding pleased. "And it's all thanks to you." His face grew sombre. "I really appreciate everything you did to find her. I don't know what I'd have done if . . . if . . ." He trailed off.

"It's what the Pet Finders are for," Tristan said cheerfully. "We're glad we could help – although next time perhaps she could pick a smaller warehouse to get lost in!"

David smiled. "I hope there *isn't* a next time," he said. "But if there is, I'll know who to ring." He nodded towards the arena. "Windwhistle did well. I must go and congratulate Amanda." He waved at them before turning towards the entrance to the ring.

"I bet Honey wins next year," Andi said.

"Me too," Natalie agreed.

Tristan raised his can of drink. "Well done the Pet Finders, for solving not one but two more cases!"

Natalie agreed. "Not to mention earning free makeovers for Buddy and Jet!" she reminded them.

Andi high-fived each of her friends in turn. "Here's to Honey, Zebedee, and most of all, to us!"

book 1

THE PET FINDERS CLUB

Come Back, Buddy!

Do you love animals?
Has your pet ever gone missing?

Well meet Andi, Tristan and Natalie —
The Pet Finders Club. Animals don't stay
lost for long with them hot on the trail!

Andi and her mum have just moved
from Texas to Aldcliffe. To make the
situation worse, her beloved Jack Russell,
Buddy, had gone missing! How will he
find his way home in a new town?

And more importantly, how is Andi going
to cope in a new place without him?